"July 30th: Fury ar

A.M. Beng

Arcana Intellego

Original title: 30 DE JULIO, UN DÍA DE FURIA Y VENGANZA

Spanish First edition. July 31, 2020.

 ISBN: 978-1393894421

Written by A. M. Bengoa.

To the inhabitants of Mexico City, a violent, filthy, yet simultaneously imposing and beautiful place.

The content of this story is born of imagination, narrating violent events without glorifying or promoting crime in any form. The name signing this book is a pseudonym used in the *Mexico Under Fire* series.

Periférico Sur, Mexico City. 11:54 AM. July 30th.

The rain, with its fat, cold, acidic drops, cascades over my shoulders. I pause for a second, realizing my head is soaked and dripping, obscuring my vision. Shaking myself like a dog, I try to rid my hair of the water trapped within, but it's useless. The inevitable vapor from my breath fogs up my glasses, further blurring my sight. A faint whitish haze invades the lenses, irritating me, breaking my concentration. Frustrated, I shake my head again and mutter a few expletives under my breath. That persistent fog blurs my vision, so I rip off my glasses and scrub them furiously, my growing desperation stirring nausea deep in my gut. Tension courses through my veins, and a chaotic storm brews in my mind, making it impossible to process the thoughts flashing through my head.

The air reeks of wet earth, the smell flooding my nostrils and dragging me back to childhood memories of playing in the muddy yard at my grandmother's house. Meanwhile, the polluted smog has been pushed down by the rain, replaced by the unmistakable scent of earth and water—the aroma of one cycle ending and another beginning. The contamination in the rainwater has transformed it into an acidic liquid, burning everything in its path. The smog has ceded ground to the pervasive, dominating dampness, creeping into every corner without ceremony. Like the atmosphere of an orchard in April, where budding flowers battle the weeds threatening to choke them, it's a reminder that every cycle holds a balance between beauty and ugliness, good and evil. Ironically, though this cyclical interplay is evident to all, few of us wield any control over it.

I breathe deeply, trying to focus on what lies ahead, but my efforts are fruitless, ridiculous even, leaving me with a dry mouth and mounting impatience.

A mixture of frustration and nausea drives me to the brink. My hands begin to tremble, and it's harder than I expected to accept the truth: the person standing there, motionless in the rain, uncomfortable and under immense pressure—is not me. It cannot be. I reflect silently, realizing that just weeks ago, I wouldn't have felt this way. How did I end up taking this cursed job? Something within me seems to slip away, as light and fleeting as water evaporating into the air.

I take another breath, trying to steady myself. I think about the horizon—one I presume exists beyond my fogged-up view. I imagine the countless droplets soaking the asphalt, visualizing their density and rhythm as they fall. I search for some sort of refuge within myself, questioning who or what owns my thoughts. For a moment, I hesitate, unsure. Maybe I've never been sure. My entire life, it's felt like I wasn't the master of all my actions, nor the architect of my destiny. Right now, I feel disconnected from my "self," scattered, melting away with the rain that continues to patter lightly against the pavement.

A sudden tremor runs through my right hand—a cramp, cold and alien. I watch it quiver, as if possessed by an external force intent on severing it from my will. Yet, I stop and remind myself that in the world of sensations, I can regain control. Silently, I command my hand to stop trembling, subduing it, asserting that it belongs to me and is bound to my will alone. Still, the cold sweat trickling down my back and beading on my forehead distracts me. I take another deep breath, but something inside me resists, contradicting me.

With the back of the hand that had been trembling just moments ago, I wipe the beads of sweat glistening on my broad forehead. It feels as though my forehead is no longer mine—a field invaded by countless droplets of sweat, alien and unfamiliar. It doesn't even resemble the one I had years ago. My contracted, aching back feels equally foreign, like a borrowed body part grafted onto a soul that no longer resembles the one it once was.

A dreadful thought grips me, disrupting my focus on the "plan." I am not myself. In front of me are a pair of trembling, unsteady hands. They feel alien, amorphous, unrecognizable. These are not the hands I remember—nimble and capable. My hands would never have trembled before undertaking an operation. They would have remained calm, steady, as I used to be. Yet, here they are, within my reach, ready to obey.

I stretch out my right hand, opening and closing it as a shiver courses through me. Biting my lip, I confirm it still hurts to do so. I extend my left hand and mimic the motions of the right, like a strange exercise meant to reassure myself. Both respond perfectly, their functionality intact, though lingering doubt gnaws at me.

There was a moment when my mind went blank, and I can't quite grasp why. Before my wide, black eyes, encircled by dark, heavy rings of exhaustion, lies a scattered collection of countless small pieces. I question whether they're even real—pieces of a puzzle I no longer intend to solve. They sit arranged in a predetermined order, configured by an uncertain destiny, one I have no right to analyze, much less comprehend.

I take another breath and start cataloging my discoveries, becoming acutely aware of my being and its physical boundaries. I retell myself the story I always rehearse before starting a job, grounding myself in its familiarity, even as doubt and alienation creep in.

I will begin my tale; I return from my wanderings and, as I pause to reconstruct a new narrative of events, trying to bring some clarity to the scene, I first become aware of the "existence" of the vast twelve-lane highway stretching endlessly into the horizon. At times, it feels as though it dissolves into the infinite banality of the everyday, coexisting with the scattered pieces of an impossible puzzle. It seems locked in a futile dialogue, as though demanding answers from infinity, yet receiving none.

Undoubtedly, this is something akin to a road meant to lead the faithful to a promised heaven, especially those naive enough to believe in the guiding hand of a divine force controlling the grand machinery of existence. This road, it seems, is for the timid and the trembling, for the mediocres and the weak-willed who cling to the hope of a diluted paradise—a place destined to devour them through their own inexorable fate. It is the realm of gods with countless names, gods who, tragically, have perished and faded into obscurity amidst the savage waiting for an answer that will never come. There is a certain kindness in these notions, a fleeting benevolence regarding gods and their fearful followers, but they are little more than sparks of goodness that lead nowhere.

I take a deep breath, managing, for a brief moment, to focus. I construct some semblance of structure within the depths of my mind. An interoceptive network connects to some indeterminate part of my hypothalamus, and eventually, the neuronal synapses allow me to grasp my thoughts. It feels as though I can finally connect. I must do so—it's part of the rules we impose on ourselves to survive in this "business."

I resolve to conclude my account of the events while steadying my breathing, attempting to slow the rhythm, to control the amount of carbon dioxide escaping my nose. Even as my skin continues to release faint clouds of vapor, my glasses gradually stop fogging, and at last, I can see clearly through them. As my vision sharpens, I confirm what I had only imagined before. Everything—and everyone—moves forward. The constant motion pulls me into it, if only momentarily. I watch the flow of traffic, breathe deeply, and sense that something lies beyond the mountains framing the scene. A desire wells within me—a wish to be somewhere other than here.

I glance around, trying to impose order on the elements of this uncomfortable space. A strange calm settles over me as I realize I *exist*. I become conscious of the reality of objects—the trees and palms swaying in the wind. I watch their rhythmic dance while the soundscape is dominated by the hum of passing cars, those multicolored metallic fragments on rubber tires, their friction against the black pavement producing a muted cacophony. White lines, ephemeral and strict, divide and categorize them. Inside these moving shells, engines hum with heat and purpose, propelling their passengers toward unknown destinations along a road without end. It is a concentric, transparent path, teeming with inanimate objects in motion, subject to the whims of those who govern them.

The pieces of the puzzle operate like a mechanism driven by a series of counterweights, forces locked in constant tension, propelled by energy that arises from combustion and transformation. These ephemeral components fuse with new ones, evaporate, or grind against each other, and it is this endless interplay that keeps this microcosm in perpetual motion. Sometimes, the pieces wear out and break... they die, like stars exploding and burning out. I can't help but feel that if, by some chance, everything came to a halt, even for a moment, the entire system would collapse, and the world would tear itself apart.

Perhaps that's why, day after day, all the characters summoned to this ballet reenact the same tedious, monotonous scene, turning it into a routine devoid of meaning. It is an act of repetition that gradually hollows them out, though they never notice. They are incapable of breaking free, of opposing the rule of consumption that dictates the ticking seconds of their existence. They accept the monotony, trapped in its dull rhythm. Only life's traumatic events seem to jolt them awake, if only briefly. Sometimes, these very events are what allow those of us who are different to escape the system. To be different always makes you stronger, more resilient, more resistant.

Invariably, the humans who play their roles on this stage walk with hollow heads filled with a ceaseless hum, like the buzz of flies circling garbage. It drones on incessantly, disturbing their thoughts, drowning out their inner voices. This compels them to follow the crowd without reflection, unaware of the error in doing so, until it silently consumes them, bit by bit. At the same time, it fills them with despair, trapping them in endless, directionless circles. They move forward, if "forward" is even the right word for what they do.

I suppress the impulse to run, to flee this place, to sprint until my strength is spent and I collapse onto the ground, lying there as my labored breath brings me closer to the final act—ready to embrace death as my new and eternal companion. Ah, how fortunate are those who find something everlasting. Once again, I take a deep breath, confronting myself, admitting that this is all I know how to do. I remind myself of the vital rule: to do what I am good at.

The Mexico City freeway is a circuit encircling the urban sprawl far from the historic heart of the "City of Palaces." It has neither a beginning nor an end—you can traverse it endlessly and never find a starting point or a destination. I force myself to overcome the discomfort, and slowly, I begin to see more clearly. The highway is crowded with cars, as always, and I tirelessly study the phenomena around me. The vehicles move at a steady pace, something remarkable considering the time of day and the sheer number of blank minds in this space—automatons wrapped in metal shells, producing a sound like the hum of an agitated beehive.

I take a deep breath, trying to confirm my existence—that I occupy a volume in both time and space, that I have the ability to control my destiny and, perhaps, even the destiny of others. I grasp that responsibility with trembling hands, forcing them to steady as I regain control of myself. I think, and I attempt to delve deeper—to understand what they are thinking. Yet I withdraw from this "game" before I can unravel the workings of their minds, before I can even be certain of their existence. It must be impossible to attain such clarity. The only thing I am sure of is that, in this moment, I hold their fate in my hands—whether they exist or not.

A feeling of doubt washes over me as I realize how those people—the ones moving about with such confidence in their own existence—manage to keep surviving. They seem to think it's enough to always be in each other's way, constantly obstructing one another as they drift aimlessly, governed by invisible forces far greater than themselves. They're like caricatured mice trapped within the massive gears of an all-encompassing machine, scrambling in vain to escape the system. Yet the absurdity becomes most apparent when they block each other's paths, collide clumsily, and engage in unnecessary confrontations, all in an effort to assert a nonexistent sense of superiority. Others attempt to prove the unprovable, yet not one of them possesses a shred of reason.

I force myself to move quickly, silently rationalizing: *They must be doing all this with some malicious intent*. Or perhaps these "actors on the stage" are more like ants in chaos, disoriented by the destruction of their anthill. Insects, at least, cannot forgive themselves for destroying their own civilization—it's as though they perceive themselves as a threat. Humans, on the other hand, fail to grasp that one person's fate is inextricably linked to another's. They overlook the fundamental meaning of civilization: collaboration, not cheap displays of irrational superiority. In truth, nothing we believe in truly exists—it's all a fiction.

Again, I take a deep breath, as if trying to convince myself that more oxygen might make me feel less uneasy, less nauseated. It doesn't work. There's a discomfort in my stomach, like a knot stretching from my throat down to the beginning of my large intestine. Still, I can feel my heartbeat—its rhythm pulsing through my wrists, thumping in my temples. I wish I were somewhere else, as a drop of sweat mixes with the rain running down my back, sending a shiver through me. I position myself precisely, check the time, consult the weather. The air is still a problem—I know because the palm trees are swaying westward.

Memories crash over me like a wave. I think about how, long ago, I wasn't "so aware" of this—of existence, of the system's mechanisms. Back then, I achieved better results because everything seemed easier. I didn't have to think about the implications of my actions. Maybe everything changed during the years I withdrew from the "business."

It's clear that coming back is no simple task, and I wouldn't have done it—wouldn't have wanted to return—had I not realized one day that I was going to die.

It's true. In the end, we all die, and it hardly matters when it happens. You'll end up lying somewhere, stiff and cold, eventually becoming food for the worms. For me, the idea came out of nowhere, an uninvited thought that invaded my mind and refused to let go. It took hold of everything I've done since. Like birds perched on fountains or puddles, they won't leave no matter what. They splash around, bathe, drink, and slowly ruin the water with their droppings—without permission, without care for how far they've flown. That's how death came to me, suddenly and without warning.

All the dead I've known seemed to sense their end long before the fatal moment arrived. Some wrote about it in their diaries, others confided in their spouses. Some distanced themselves, disappearing until a premonition crept into the hearts of those close to them, who then somehow knew they were gone—or so their families claim. Some sketched their fate in notebooks, and there were even those who dreamt of themselves as both dead and immortal. My brother once told me that if anything ever happened to him, I should leave, flee, run until I reached a place where no one knew me, where I could start a new life. Looking back, I think I should have listened to him.

But I didn't. Instead, I once learned of a painter who, throughout his life, painted images of his own death. Yet when he felt it approaching, he created a painting of a newborn protected by a woman. He later organized an auction of all his works, and after they had been sold, he confessed to the buyers that he had never feared death—until he realized it was inevitable. My brother knew it was likely that one day he wouldn't come home, and that if he did, it would be in a box from which he'd never emerge.

Painters and sculptors, I think, should make it a rule to hide from death when they feel it nearing. Moreover, they should adhere to the only acceptable formula in such cases: write a manual to preserve the true meaning of their art. Without it, they risk letting others interpret their work, leading to an incalculable confusion. In the end, art becomes speculative and fragmented. By this, I mean that criticism is nothing more than an attempt to appropriate the judgment of an interpretative experience. Critics always aim to tell us what to feel and how to feel it. They try to understand what others create but fail, expressing themselves in convoluted, pretentious ways—always far removed from what the artist originally intended to convey. Worse, they are people who never knew the deceased, who never spoke to them. I've never understood criticism, and I find it despicable.

Perhaps that's why I neither write nor draw, much less paint or sculpt, or engage in any of those pursuits. I do something entirely different, something simple yet tragic, dramatic in a way that feels almost theatrical, with a touch of suspense, and undoubtedly poetic and artistic. Those who know little about this "work" often think of it as spiritual, as a bridge between two worlds. I avoid confusing myself with such notions or entertaining ideas that might haunt me. But if I were to explain it to someone, I would simply say that my work cleanses souls and expiates the wrongs of the world. Some of my colleagues prefer to interact with individuals who meet a certain profile—those who've committed heinous acts against good people. Personally, I find such intrusions unacceptable. What I know for sure is that what I do leaves very little memory behind: I kill people.

I do it for a paycheck, though sometimes I've done it for favors. When I was younger, I killed for power and submission. I followed orders and gave them. There is always an immense exchange of power in what I do. Regret? None at all. I am part of the most fundamental cycle of life. Spiritually, I see myself as the one who schedules appointments with the divine. Personally, I like to think this will score me some points toward my own fate. If I ever stand before Saint Peter, I'll proudly tell him I personally sent many souls his way.

I must focus. I repeat this to myself as if to avoid forgetting it—or perhaps to seek a sliver of forgiveness within me. As I do, I fix my gaze on the backdrop of the scene, on the paraphernalia before me. It's all part of a reality others are aware of, a reality where I am but a speck of dust, a faint blip on the heart monitor of someone with tachycardia—a fleeting moment that will soon vanish from memory.

I think of the asymmetric, rain-soaked landscape before me, noting how pointlessly it's filled with rocky formations and absurd mountains with trees in the distance—a distance I don't recognize, one I frantically search for in my memories. Those trees, equally absurd, green and dense, form a range that vainly attempts to blend into the rest of the scenery. Terrible clouds stretch across the gray sky and the vast *sierra* surrounding me, their ominous shadows suspended in a delicate composition that weeps rain. The sound of the falling drops distracts me, pulling me back to the present.

Though I fix my eyes on a lost point again, my thoughts swirl. For a moment, I nearly let my gaze return to the sparse vegetation of the median strip: sickly pines and eucalyptus, half-grown grass, and the wind breaking the silence. Now the raindrops fall directly on my face, so I turn my body to shield myself from the rain.

In the air, pollution, silent and insidious like any noxious killer, drifts skyward, carried by the dark clouds that rise, imposing and unreachable. They traverse the heavens, meandering along their own path amidst the haze of uncertainty, their grayness refusing to dissipate. At the end of this long journey between the city and its hills, forces collide, unleashing rain, torrential downpours, and hail. Rivers swell violently, morphing into destructive torrents, while on the streets, water rises abruptly. People scatter, the streets and avenues empty, and the city grows eerily silent, as if awaiting something inevitable.

The citizens retreat, hiding as though the water's wrath commands a subdued response from the anthill that is this chaotic metropolis. In my mind's eye, I involuntarily picture people running, seeking refuge under makeshift shelters. I allow myself a moment to close my eyes and take a deep breath. I see it—a once-mighty city. But now, I imagine it from a great distance, alien and unrecognizable, this chaotic, cruel place overrun by a pestilence I can no longer comprehend. Lately, I find myself lost within it, disoriented by inexplicable silences that echo through the cries of ensnared, rigid souls.

I hide, crouched uncomfortably behind the low wall of a pedestrian bridge—a narrow crossing used more by stray dogs than by humans. In this city, where those who roam freely are few, it feels like everything is falling apart. I remain curled up in the confined space that squeezes me, tucked where air, water, and sky converge—a forgotten nook I've claimed as my own. Here, in silence, I sift through the lessons I've absorbed, mechanically whispering a prayer to bring forth the memories I've chosen to recall. Even if most of those memories are lies or frivolities, they sustain me. This is how life is built, how one coexists with the "work"—lying to oneself and crafting memories of things that never happened.

My knees ache, pressed against the soaked ground, which is slowly flooding. My hands, encased in black gloves, have stopped trembling entirely. They feel alien, stiff, yet deceptively obedient. I've stayed this way, watchful and stealthy, for more than forty-five minutes, resisting the urge to light a cigarette, to look at the sky for signs the rain might stop, to escape the gnawing unease. I've denied myself the thought that I am not this person, that the figure crouched on this wretched bridge is someone else—a vile, pernicious stranger. And yet, in this strange identity, there lies a creature capable of soaring beyond its station.

Above all, I've resisted the overpowering desire to flee, refusing to let fate fulfill its brutal mandate—that I should take the life of an innocent and kidnap a stranger.

I exhale deeply, aware that I carry out this task with unease, with a faint remorse that makes guilt stir within me. This is wrong—I should feel nothing. I must not allow any emotion to interfere with my ability to act decisively. Yet, I maintain a façade of serenity, my focus sharp, watching the traffic on the road where my target will soon pass. The commitment to this mission restrains me, frustrating and constraining my thoughts. In the meantime, I rehearse, over and over, the reasons—few or many—that have led me here.

I conclude that, in this space—one I inhabit as an invader, a being composed of an alien substance, an amalgam of intrinsic atoms—I am, as I have always been throughout my story, an imprudent intruder. A collection of carbon, calcium, and diverse elements, I wait silently, watching for a black vehicle. A large one, luxurious and gleaming, even on rainy days like this. I glance at my watch, feeling the tension mount, fearing the second hand might stop, suspending everything in an impossible pause. At moments, my mind imagines scenarios that cannot occur, though their improbability doesn't stop the dread they inspire.

The thought invades me, terrifies me, throwing my senses into disarray. My head spins, the idea swells into unimaginable proportions. If it were to manifest, it would bring about my own destruction. Should time freeze, I'd sink into the endless stress of inaction, my mind crushed by the sheer eternity of nothingness. Perhaps my heart would give out, or I'd leap from this bridge where I now crouch. The thought terrifies me—that I might falter, fail to pull the trigger. But it's never happened before, and there's no reason it should now.

From the black vehicle—whose license plates, occupants, origins, and destination I know well—I will emerge as the one who decides their fates. I know little of the car itself, just scattered details of the man who drives it. Sergio Ramos is his name. Beyond that, I know nothing—perhaps he has children, a wife, a mother. With him is an older man. Whether he is good or evil, a killer or a saint, I cannot say. I do not know if he has tortured or simply lived. These judgments are irrelevant.

My task is to choose their destinies. Nothing will prevent me from doing so. I know the car will approach along this major avenue, the grandest in the country. This event, though it will surely be remembered, is not why I act. Not anymore. Long ago, I had reasons—fame, fortune, the fleeting motivations of a hired gun. Now, such ambitions are meaningless. This is not about gracing tabloid covers or earning infamy. My employer, though unknown to me, seeks something far greater: to send a message. A message of terror.

The intent is clear. Tomorrow morning, over breakfast, the public will shiver reading headlines that stoke fear, nausea, and despair. News broadcasts will showcase the carnage—fire, destruction, death. My employer wishes to ignite dread in every viewer, to remind them that unseen forces wield absolute control over their lives.

Though I do not know my employer, I suspect they possess power. Their motives seem rooted in demonstrating dominance, ensuring their message resonates deeply. Such displays serve a purpose: to instill fear, the foundation of respect in this business. Over time, you learn that true respect rarely exists—only fear does. This truth pervades every level of society. Respect is an illusion; fear is the universal currency.

For outsiders, the mechanics of abduction remain incomprehensible. Why we do it, how we select our targets—these are mysteries to them. The answers, though complex, serve precise functions. The key lies in the "informant." This individual infiltrates the habits and routines of the target, compiling detailed reports on their daily life and their closest associates. Without the informant, none of this would be possible. Information is the most valuable asset of our age.

Thanks to our informant's meticulous dossier, I know the older man we're about to take has just left an important breakfast meeting. There is no room for doubt; we've verified every detail. Success hinges on reducing errors, as mistakes are costly. Occasionally, chance interferes—timing goes awry, the target slips away. But even then, the process repeats. A new report is drafted, the plan adjusted. To minimize these risks, someone—an unknown voice on the phone—confirms the facts. "The package is en route," they say, or, "He changed his route," or, "He stayed longer than expected." These updates keep the operation on course, ensuring the inevitability of what is to come.

When no one calls you, you're forced to make the call yourself. There's only time for one question—it's always simple, often obvious: *Are they headed to the meeting yet? Has the gentleman left the breakfast? Love, are you coming with me to such and such a place?* The goal is to not draw attention. You adapt your actions based on the information received. It's a complex job, one that relies on trusting certain parties—most of whom you don't even know by their real names. This has been the way of "The Uncle's" organization for over forty years. It's how we've been trained.

Someone called us with information about our target. The old man is coming, just as expected, in the black vehicle. Our contact responded exactly as we wanted: kidnapping. It's not the kind of operation you can carry out alone. It depends on countless moving parts, like a massive machine that turns us into a pack of stealthy mice. To ensure our "guest" attends the meeting, invisible forces must be applied. For a man of his age to be coerced without resistance, his friends, colleagues, or even his lover might already be complicit. In some way or another, they've pushed him to take the Periférico Ring Road, leaving him no choice but to follow the path we've set for him. It's only a matter of time now.

Tomorrow, the headlines won't ask *how* he was ambushed. Instead, they'll ask *who*. Who could be so twisted, so malevolent, as to commit such a crime in broad daylight, with thousands of witnesses? Who wanted the disappearance of "So-and-So" to be so glaringly obvious? In truth, no one cares about his name. Let's be honest—they're not even interested in the motive. What grabs their attention is *who* did it, *who* ordered it. Then, the so-called moral voices will ask: *Who are we at the mercy of? What kind of scoundrels threaten our children's safety?* Some will pontificate over breakfast tables, while others, cloaked in their private darkness, will agonize over the question: *What kind of monster is on the loose?* And the guiltiest among them will wonder: *Could this happen to me or my loved ones?*

People shouldn't fear—not if they've stayed on the straight and narrow. Bad things can happen to good people, of course, but not as often. As for the journalists, especially the ones anchoring the nightly news, they'll label this act as heinous, cowardly, and despicable. That's just how journalists are—they think they're qualified to judge what they don't understand.

What few will admit, though they know it, is that many of those who pay for those sensational adjectives are the same ones who hire people like me to do this. For people like me, labels are irrelevant. Besides, lately, the questions these reporters ask are ridiculously naive, as if they hope to enlighten their audience. That's why I prefer print journalists. Sometimes, they manage to grasp the essence of things—though never completely. When they speak the truth, they suffer for it. When they stay silent, they suffer too. But at least it's clear they understand.

As I wait here, crouched, diminished, and soaked like a stray dog, my thoughts churn violently. They ricochet around my mind like wild fireballs, rarely returning to their place. It's like a puzzle with too many missing pieces—disorder and chaos reign supreme. Those gaps, I think, are memories, wounds, and the absence of certain people. They're blank spaces I've never been able to fill. Lately, they've started to make sense, just like much of my life has in these recent days. Days that led me to decide to return to "the business."

This tangled web of ideas makes my head throb. Out-of-place, illogical memories cloud my vision and judgment. Once again, I'm reminded that I'm here without passion, merely to complete a task—just another job like any other. A job for which I'll be paid a fee, a salary.

Perhaps you don't understand—allow me to explain. At first, taking someone else's life is something you approach with great seriousness. It's not easy. It requires practice, honed over years and through mechanical repetition. Over time, it becomes second nature, blending with a certain cynicism. The guilt fades little by little until you reach a point where the challenge isn't the act itself but remembering how many souls you've sent to the grave. To reach that point, you need to see things from a different perspective.

Some people eat from the trash to survive. Others live by lies, wearing titles that range from actors to politicians. There are those who sell their bodies. Most of them do what they do out of necessity, pushed by a system that forced them into roles they never wanted to play.

When I started viewing my work through this lens, I realized that I was just another laborer. A worker with a wage, like any other. An ordinary man selling his time to a boss—a faceless owner of lives and minutes whom I'll never meet but to whom I trade my services for money. From this boss, I expect no kindness. There will be no gratitude for my fine work, no social benefits or legal protections, no vacation days or retirement savings. None of those comforts. And yet, one survives by accepting these conditions, because there's simply no other choice.

If you prefer a more sensitive explanation, let me pause to clarify further. The comforts and pleasantries I just mentioned mean little to the worker who, reduced to a tool, is hired solely by the forces of supply and demand. We, too, are a kind of artist. Our craft is unique, specialized. We are selected as one might choose a virtuoso musician—someone who, once on stage, creates a masterpiece on their instrument. But let's not get caught up in frivolities.

The truth is, both the worker and the assassin grow accustomed to lives devoid of hope or recognition. One is despised, the other feared—and sometimes even admired. Suspended in this limbo for years, they exist in parallel, enduring the same hollow reality.

As for me, I no longer care for recognition. I'm past even the faint hope for the illusion of respect from an affable boss. Perhaps the one who hired me is the only reason I hold this weapon in my hands. But the truth is, survival demands it. If you don't know what I mean, ask the thousands of teenagers who live as mules or who kill for a paycheck—just as I once started.

This is a city of rage and destruction, where survival is a fight every single day.

Some say that killing and dying are strikingly similar. Sometimes, I think that when you kill someone, a part of you dies with them. It feels as if that part of you sets off on an unknown journey, perhaps following that person—someone whose full name you never even knew. You'll never find out if, on the morning you gunned them down, they said goodbye to their spouse, blessed their children, or made peace with their mother after leaving home angry at the ruin of their life.

You won't know if anyone will mourn their death. You'll never know how much harm they caused others—if such a thing can even be measured. That part of you that dies leaves a void. You may foolishly think you can fill it with love, but you'd be wrong. The only thing that fills it is hate—a hate accompanied by a pain that never leaves, a permanent ache.

Sometimes, you learn things. The person you killed in that dark alley was a murderer, like you. Maybe he violated a child. Perhaps he mutilated a man. And so, you convince yourself that you've restored some balance—returned a sliver of life to the one who suffered at the hands of the bastard you put in a cold, gray metal coffin. You tell yourself it's an exchange: you take the life of a stranger to save a little dignity for the victim. For a fleeting moment, you feel good. You think you've redeemed someone from their torment. But deep down, you know that one day, it will be your turn. You won't escape it—just like the one who avenges your offenses won't either.

And so, half-dead, you keep moving forward, because what else is there? Today, I'm here, following my fate.

The raindrops fall relentlessly from the sky. I look at my black gloves, a mix of fabric and leather. I glance at my watch to confirm the second hand is moving. The countdown is almost over. But in the meantime, I want to recount a piece of a story, one I replay in my mind.

Telling stories—that's something I've done before, perhaps since I was a child. I would have loved for someone to listen. I could have made a life out of sharing tales about the world. But that wasn't the path chosen for me.

Let me warn you: this isn't a good story. It's a real one, almost tangible. It's the tragedy of all of us born into a time and a generation consigned to the forgotten pages of history. It's so common you could find it replicated, almost identical, on any street corner where children beg for food, on any bus where shirtless teens sell gum, or in the lifeless gaze of the young man commuting beside you, his hair unwashed and his hope lost. It's repeated endlessly—maybe even within your own home, in the life of the adolescent helping with chores, or, who knows, in your own child.

No one tells their stories anymore. There's never time. No one pauses to reflect on what we've become.

The weapon in my hands is my tool of the trade—a means to craft my art. It has been since the first time I held a gun. That was long ago—so long, I can't recall the day I first used one to take another human life. I've spent countless sleepless nights trying to pinpoint when I killed without fear. But that part of me that died must have taken those memories with it.

Perhaps it was someone insignificant—a stranger who defied me during a petty robbery. I can't remember, and it eats away at me—the guilt and the fear. If the soul exists, where will mine end up?

I know there must have been a first time. There's a first time for everything, good or bad. But my memories are blurred—vague scenes shrouded in darkness. I can't clearly trace how I got here, to this point in my life, or why I ended up doing what I do: intimidating and dominating others.

People say I overthink things, that it's all destiny. They claim our fates are etched into the lines on our palms, and we must accept them.

When I started this, there were no other options—especially not where I was born. My name is Alejandro Mejía, though almost no one remembers the name my parents gave me. At least my mother does. Most people call me *El Pasa*. They've done so for decades. It's because of my skin—olive-toned, much like the color of my gun: a Stealth Recon Scout rifle, imported from the north, though they like to deny it. It's a short rifle, easy to conceal, which makes it ideal for missions like this.

At some point, we all retreat to the mountains. I no longer do this professionally. You could say this is a favor I'm repaying. But for a long time, I killed to survive—to eat. Back then, I preferred different weapons. My evolution as a hired killer is a long and unfortunate tale, much like most of them.

The wind isn't entirely favorable—I can tell by the swaying palms on the campus of the nearby technical university. Their restless motion gives away the gusts.

To hit a target like the one I'm after, you need three things. First, the wind must work in your favor. You need to calculate the vehicle's speed and the bullet's trajectory to ensure it reaches the "dead man." Second, and critically important, you need an escape route to avoid landing in one of those overcrowded prisons that few ever leave alive. Ironically, there's no death penalty in Mexico.

And third, most important of all: you must trust your weapon and your partner completely. Without them, you're in hell—whether or not you're dead.

It wasn't so common in the past for people to hire long-distance assassins. The trade has evolved. Back then, all you needed was a scooter, a gun, and a few bullets. You'd fire at your target, never entirely sure if you'd left them dead or alive. Targets could be caught leaving their homes, at a business lunch, or in a nightclub late at night. Sometimes, employers would even send a cheap lover to lure the target into the right place at the right time, willing to take a "little scare" for some extra cash. But things don't work that way anymore. You need to use more "brainpower" to predict behavior—especially when it comes to the rich. They're always targets but never easy ones.

The intercom buzzes; it's my partner, "El Tinaco." Nobody could tell you his real name. He's a good partner—talks little, handles the basics, stays sharp, and most importantly, asks very few questions. As I mull this over, "El Tinaco" growls some technical instructions over the radio. He'll be waiting beneath the pedestrian bridge where I've staked out. The target is coming in a black Lincoln. We've agreed on codenames for the two occupants: the driver, who isn't the main target, is called "Deadman." The main target, referred to as "Package," is a valuable old man in his sixties. An acquaintance from the past has an interest in detaining him for a while and ensuring he complies with her wishes.

According to our plan, it won't be long before the vehicle completes its journey through the central lanes. Coming from its current location just a few kilometers away, there's no escape route. The road ensures the target reaches his inevitable destination. I check my watch. Despite the light rain, I see the second hand ticking forward. I take a deep breath and mentally review the plan. Cars cruise at an average speed of 80 kilometers per hour in the central lanes.

"El Tinaco" is waiting in an old van painted with the logo of the Metropolitan Water Commission. It looks like an official vehicle performing a routine inspection of a valve box along the avenue. It's convincing enough to pass for real—especially on a rainy day like today, with puddles forming everywhere. There's an eerie tension in the air; the rain has been falling for so long, it feels endless—cold, fine, and menacing.

I place the gun on the support tripod, resting it against the railing that conceals my hideout—a spot rarely visited by pedestrians. The weather has ensured no one disturbs my operation. For good measure, we've put up yellow caution tape to deter anyone from climbing the precarious, damaged stairs of the bridge. In a city like this, no one would be surprised if even the bridges collapsed.

My hands sweat inside my black gloves. I attach the suppressor to the gun, ensuring no sound will precede the target's death. I peer through the telescopic sight and spot the black Lincoln approaching at a steady speed. I check the wind direction one last time—it's calm now, confirmed by the uniform fall of the fine rain. I inhale deeply, steadying my pulse. I tell myself it's just another job.

The telescopic sight tells me the vehicle is 1,200 meters away. I'll have only seconds to adjust all the necessary calculations for the shot and hit the driver squarely in the chest. These are the crucial moments when experience guides instinct. With the sight aimed slightly ahead of the car's trajectory, I gently squeeze the trigger. The bullet travels fiercely, hitting the driver in the chest.

Half a second later, I pull my eye from the scope and see the chaos unfold as expected. The black vehicle crashes into the central divider of the high-speed lanes, not with great force but just enough to come to a gradual stop. The driver, either dead or gravely injured, slumps lifelessly over the wheel. Two vehicles following closely behind collide with the Lincoln. A red sports car adds to the pile-up, blocking two additional lanes of the central thoroughfare.

My partner maneuvers the old van as close as possible to the crash site, crossing a small median with trees separating the central lanes. Cars slow down, some drivers confused, others alarmed. All they could have seen was the faint flash of my gun, followed by the Lincoln's inescapable crash. The ensuing pile-up has partially blocked the freeway, and the chaos spreads as drivers honk and skid to a halt, trying to escape the disaster.

I rush down the stairs as "El Tinaco" steps out of the van with his semi-automatic weapon. He fires several shots at the armored windshield of the Lincoln to obscure the trajectory of my sniper round, making it harder for investigators to trace. Reaching the Lincoln, he forces open the back door. Even through the rain, I can see him drag out an elderly man with white hair, wearing a beige shirt and tobacco-colored pants. With his left hand, he restrains the man, while with his right, he fires another round into the headrest of the driver's seat.

I start the van's engine and take the driver's seat. Moments later, I hear the sliding door shut and the gruff commands of "El Tinaco," signaling it's time to leave. The freeway, now gridlocked by the wreck, slows any response from emergency crews. I hit the gas, and the battered van groans as we speed away.

We leave the scene of chaos and destruction behind—a wake of fire, blaring horns, and general panic. In the distance, sirens wail: ambulances, police cars, and fire trucks scrambling to the scene. "El Tinaco," the Package, and I escape in our decrepit van. No one truly understands what just happened—a brazen daylight abduction in front of countless witnesses, none of whom could offer any concrete testimony.

Twenty blocks ahead, another vehicle with similar characteristics is waiting for us. The van with the official markings will be set ablaze to prevent state authorities from tracing our steps, at least not as quickly as they might hope. This also ensures that any DNA evidence, such as hair strands, cannot be used to identify us. Other men are responsible for burning the van while we continue toward the designated site to deliver the "package."

The most challenging part of the operation was already behind us. As we drive, I reflect on the hours ahead. "El Tinaco" and I will transport the "package" to the Sierra de Santa Catarina, where we'll leave him without further complications in the "location." The site is notoriously difficult to access, even for the highest-ranking authorities. It's clear that the elderly man in our custody is a big shot.

Upon reaching the second vehicle, "El Tinaco" subdued the victim, knocking him unconscious with his fists and well-honed experience. Now, my partner takes the wheel, steering us through our escape route, leaving no room for error.

Senate of the Republic, Mexico City, 12:29 PM, July 30th

From the elevator doors on the seventh floor of the Senate building, two figures emerged. Dressed in dark blue—the classic uniform of Federal Police officers—they appeared slightly disoriented as they approached the first desk they saw. They asked the secretary of the right-wing party coordinator a question. She stood up, gesturing toward the office at the far end of the floor. One of the men moved quickly, his face displaying an expression that seemed oddly out of place.

At the end of the hallway, Rosario Shafter, secretary to Senator Fernando Pérez Irigoyen, watched them approach with a mix of curiosity and unease. She noted how the two men walked silently, their faces carrying the stoic, foreboding look typical of officers about to deliver bad news. Without understanding why, Rosario gripped her pen tightly, her fingers reddening before turning slightly white. She avoided their gaze for brief moments, focusing instead on the distant sound of their footsteps, growing louder as they neared.

When the two men finally reached her desk, Rosario looked up and asked calmly, maintaining an air of composure, "How can I help you?" Her tone was steady, her breath controlled, though her heart raced slightly.

The men identified themselves, confirming what their uniforms already suggested. They were commanders from the Federal Police's Anti-Kidnapping Division. They explained they had urgent information to convey personally to Senator Pérez Irigoyen.

Rosario hesitated for a moment, then reached for the white phone on her desk. Dialing a series of numbers, she held the receiver to her ear, glancing briefly into the deep, dark eyes of one of the officers before instinctively averting her gaze to an unfocused point in space. In a mechanical voice, she uttered a few words and then waited.

She was calling the Senator's personal assistant, a short-statured man named Joaquín—the only person who could locate Fernando Pérez Irigoyen.

Fer, as he had always been called at home, in school, and even now in the political arena, had risen quickly and spectacularly to the Senate.

His career had surged like foam on a wave. Some attributed his meteoric ascent to good fortune and a favorable star, while others speculated darker theories, whispers of favors owed to powerful narcotics lords. People talked and theorized more than they should, as they often do. Regardless of the source of his success, to his schoolmates, Fernando Pérez Irigoyen was a charismatic, young, and successful politician. Affable, humorous, and highly social, many believed these traits were the secret to his rapid success. Over time, he cultivated numerous connections with the clear intent of leveraging them for business opportunities. This web of relationships, paired with his political aptitude, had propelled him into his Senate role. From a young age, he had been adept at forming advantageous relationships, and as he matured, he simply had to decide where best to invest his time.

Since taking office as a senator, he had revitalized numerous dormant reforms. Most recently, he had set his sights on the telecommunications sector, where his political skill had enabled the passage of measures targeting monopolistic service providers. This earned him a reputation as a rising star in politics. His face graced the covers of business and political magazines almost monthly, and there wasn't a week without an interview in a major national newspaper. Television appearances, though, were his favorite—a secret indulgence.

On a personal level, Fernando was recently single. His wife had requested a divorce just days after his swearing-in as senator. The split only added to his mystique, transforming him into the coveted bachelor of Mexican politics and a top contender for his party's presidential nomination—the strongest opposition to the ruling faction with a realistic chance of securing the presidency. Many saw him as the prototype of the modern young politician, a label he sometimes embraced and openly declared.

As the "eligible bachelor" and a viable presidential candidate, he also engaged in philanthropic and humanitarian work, further enriching his expansive portfolio of connections. He cultivated these relationships methodically, ensuring they would be useful when the time came. His goal was to elevate these ties to a more intimate level, strategically aligning himself with various power players to enhance his position.

From his days studying law at the National University's Faculty of Law in Ciudad Universitaria, Fernando had been in the spotlight. He and a group of exceptional students attracted attention, not just for their academic performance but also for their ties to families with deep political roots, ready to reclaim power. From the beginning, people "had their eye" on Fernando—not as the leader, but as the second in command. Still, it wasn't unusual to see him surrounded by beautiful women, businessmen, ambassadors, and, most commonly, flatterers.

He had tried to position himself as the group's leader, but it never materialized. Two or three others, either due to lineage or brilliance, remained at the forefront. Fernando consoled himself by believing he didn't need to be the top figure; maintaining his presence was enough. Over the past three years, however, his dreams had all come true, culminating in his arrival at the Senate.

When Joaquín answered the phone, his response was as routine as ever—a firm refusal to interrupt the senator.

"Rosario, you know better," Joaquín said dismissively. "The senator is busy in a private meeting, and you know how he gets when I interrupt him. Call me back in fifteen minutes, and I'll see what I can do."

Rosario, however, insisted, explaining the presence of the Federal Police officers. Joaquín hesitated before finally agreeing to let them through. "Fine, put them on the line. I'll interrupt him—if he gets mad, he'll take it out on me, not you, Rosario."

He wasn't sure if he had thought or spoken those last words. Regardless, he made his way to where the senator was seated at the far end of Loma Linda, tucked away in a corner of the terrace shielded from prying eyes. Joaquín interrupted Fernando, who waved him over with a hand gesture to pass him the phone.

Seated at the table with Fernando were several businesspeople and politicians seeking advice and support from the senator. After a brief pause, Fernando Pérez Irigoyen took the phone and listened. His expression shifted dramatically as the voice on the other end spoke, the change palpable. Silence engulfed the room.

"Your father has been kidnapped," Commander Estrada informed him. "He was en route to a breakfast meeting in Pedregal after attending a charity event in Xochimilco. He never arrived at the expected location..."

The Senator stopped listening. He knew the itinerary and his father's agenda perfectly well; they had discussed it the night before, as they often did. He had even asked his father to represent him at a breakfast with a local association. Fernando knew exactly who his father would meet, why he was meeting them, and how it would unfold—he knew everything. Pérez Irigoyen reminded Commander Estrada that his father had a chauffeur, who, more than just a driver, was also his bodyguard. He also informed him that his father's car was equipped with a satellite tracking system, which would make it easy to locate.

The commander replied that using the tracking system would not be possible. He explained that the car had been destroyed on the Periférico, in the central lanes—he specified. The chauffeur, named Sergio, was dead inside the vehicle. The commander added that the incident had occurred just moments before he was speaking to the Senator, and he would wait for him at the Senate Tower to escort him to the scene. There, he would have the opportunity to explain what was being done to aid the investigation. When the conversation ended, the bureaucratic investigator referred to the attack on the Senator's father as a "tragic incident," his voice grim and somewhat gloomy as they both said their farewells.

Fer excused himself from the table, and the last person expressed his complete disapproval of the event. The Senator hurried up the stairs and rushed to the establishment's glass door. His vehicle appeared unexpectedly, followed by the cars that always escorted him. The gray Mercedes Benz, with the Senator inside, sped down Paseo de la Reforma toward the Senate, while Pérez Irigoyen's mind wandered, unable to recall the last time he had felt so uncertain about what to do. The rain was relentless as they moved forward, and somehow, a group of Federal Police patrols detected him. From the old Mexican Social Security Institute building, they began to escort him, while the Senator reminisced about his childhood and watched the rain-slicked streets grow emptier with each passing moment.

July 30th, 12:38 PM, Club de Golf "La Hacienda", Atizapán de Zaragoza.

Mariela Irigoyen de Pérez is a woman who strives to live in peace and harmony with herself. She runs five kilometers daily near the golf club where she has lived for over thirty-five years. At the core of her quest for serenity, however, is a subtle influence from Eastern meditation practices that many of her friends follow. On one occasion, she attended a Yoga class, and she was also invited to try Tai Chi. She prefers to believe that these spiritual trends have had little effect on her, as they conflict with her deeply held Catholic beliefs. Secretly, Mariela checks her horoscope in gossip magazines, though she always does so quickly and furtively, making sure no one sees her.

On one occasion, she received a flyer about an informational session on Buddhism. She read it and then threw it away, casting it aside as if holding it for even a moment were a mortal sin. Yet, the thought of attending that meeting, where Buddhist wisdom would be shared by monks from Tibet, crossed her mind. Disturbed by the idea, she crumpled the flyer and tossed it into the trash, chastising herself for considering betraying her faith and religious principles. From that moment on, she realized that the devil could hide anywhere—even in seemingly harmless advertisements.

There were countless times she had complained about the disobedience of the other women who attended the noon mass at the San Judas parish. She was particularly critical of their irreverence, their lack of true faith. These women frequented cafes that offered tarot readings, gathered to listen to horoscopes, or attended talks broadcasted on TV, claiming to offer knowledge about the future and the purification of the soul. But deep down, in a secret place within her soul—one she rarely allowed herself to visit, and only occasionally—Mariela too was intrigued by those cafes and those so-called fortune-tellers. She wondered if, in God's endless mercy, He would understand her curiosity about wanting some direction on the events that might unfold in the near future.

A few days earlier, she had visited a tarot reader, who had told her that a terrible event was approaching her life, something she needed to be very aware of. When Mariela asked if it concerned her son Fernando, the woman examined the cards and assured her it wasn't him, but rather an older man. Mariela, feeling a sigh of relief, speculated that it might be her husband Raúl who was at risk. That rainy July day, when he came home, she told him about "a dream" she had, expressing concern that he might hurt himself during his daily activities. She asked him to be extra careful, more than he usually was.

Raúl smiled, assuring her that there was nothing to worry about, that he always took double precautions, and there was no reason for anything to happen. Mariela smiled, as she always did when her husband made comments like that. He had come back after many years of being absent from their home. It was before mid-1993 when he had left one October day. He had done so because he didn't want the responsibilities life had given him—a wife, two children—because, in the end, it wasn't what he wanted. So, he left them behind, not exactly to their fate, but certainly with a hole that, over the years, had become increasingly irreplaceable. It was twelve years of silent suffering for every member of the family, each in their own way, until one day, out of the blue, he decided to return. It was unclear whether it was because his affair with the secretary he had left with had turned into a complete disaster, or because there comes an age when even the most adventurous spirit is subdued by maturity.

During the years they were apart, Raúl never stopped providing financial support—enough for Mariela to buy two properties, which she rented out. This stabilized her income and allowed her to maintain her role as a devoted mother, one who, by the way, would have given anything for her children. Deep down, the greatest pain and the only resentment she felt toward Raúl was the suffering he had caused Valeria and Fernando, their children, by abandoning them for all those long years.

Perhaps this is because she has never known problems the way others have. When she was young, she lived in a large family, her father a landowner from Guanajuato who had inherited a shoe factory and an empire in the industry. He gave her everything she needed and wanted. When she married, her husband supported her in every way. Over the years, she always depended on the good fortune of her husband, who left her properties to rent, and another significant part of her economic stability depended on her father-in-law, who took care of her and her children during her husband's absence.

In a form of repayment, she dedicated long hours to praying for others, hoping that her family would never lack for abundance and prosperity. Life continued, not in the way she had imagined, but it did continue. However, perhaps the most distinctive trait of Mariela was her concern for others, for the defenseless, for those forgotten by the hand of God. Over time, this concern grew immeasurable. In her own words, she dedicated a significant portion of her day to praying for others. She became increasingly involved in the lives of those with few resources.

For over twenty years, alongside other women from the noon mass at San Judas Church, she visited the local Barrientos prison, bringing food, warm clothing, and the word of God to the prisoners. One day, she heard a woman say that she only felt safe until the first night she was locked in the prison. This seemed inconceivable to Mariela, but it was then that she understood the Mexico she had always kept herself distanced from.

Since then, in her mind, she began imagining the countless daily struggles faced by thousands of people with limited resources. She thought of them as living in a parallel reality. When she visited, she felt a certain sorrow, crossed herself, and imagined the hardships that people living in such abandonment must endure. Sometimes, in those moments, she suffered panic attacks from having to think about so much suffering.

But her life had not been a bed of roses either. For years, she endured her husband's infidelities, always having to tolerate the assistants and secretaries who ended up being his friends and lovers, the parties that lasted days, and the unexpected trips abroad, always "for work commitments" that ended up meaning a new affair. Like the time he went to Toronto for a month to buy new energy production machinery—yet nothing ever came from Canada—or the time he went to São Paulo, where he kept all the pictures of his stay at the carnival with a stunning blonde. But it was always for the good of the company, he insisted.

In the kitchen of her house, a ceramic platter stands as a silent guardian of the family's sufferings. It is always illuminated by a wax candle, and on it, the image of the Sacred Heart of Mary watches over her thoughts, drawing her attention every time she passes by. She whispers a prayer, asking for guidance for herself and her family. The platter has been there for over thirty years, since Raúl and she were young and had united their lives.

Today, she will spend the morning cooking for lunch. It's the day off for the help, and although it's usually Hilda who takes care of this task, recently she has been acting strangely—distracted and lost. Mariela suspects that Hilda wants to quit, but how could that be possible after working with her for over twenty-five years? Hilda's daughter, Rosa, has been like a daughter to her, born when her mother began working for the family.

Sometimes, when she crosses the living room, she imagines if time could rewind. In her mind, she sees images of Fer, her youngest son, drawing on the living room sofas as a small child, or dressed in his equestrian outfit on Saturdays, practicing jumps at the French Equestrian Club, making the horses he loved to ride obey him. She realizes that time has slipped through her fingers, and all she can do is remember. At times, she has even noticed that her memories don't quite reflect how things were—surely someone could explain how she got so old so quickly.

However, she remembers that there was a turning point, a moment that divided everything into a before and after. It was that afternoon when Raúl told her and their children that he was leaving them. When that happened, Fernando clung to his father's pants, begging him not to go, while Valeria and Mariela stayed in the kitchen, devastated, surrounded by tears, in front of the same platter she had always been devoted to. It was her faith that allowed her to continue navigating life with those two children, amidst a sea of questions and few answers.

Mariela crosses herself in front of the sacred image. She doesn't do it automatically; she takes her time, giving new meaning to the act of bringing the sign of the cross to her forehead, as she does every day. Today is no exception. Behind her, she hears her daughter's footsteps descending the stairs. Valeria is heading to the monthly volunteer meeting for a congregation they both belong to. She will ask for Mariela's apology, as her mother won't be attending, because, deep down, Mariela hopes that Raúl, her "beloved" husband, will deign to eat with her. But she knows that's almost impossible. He hasn't done so even once in the past month.

Valeria, Raúl and Mariela's daughter, lives at home, even though she's been married for two years. She has a beautiful apartment in Santa Fe, but she's rarely there. Her husband travels almost six months a year, occasionally sending pictures or a text message, but little to nothing is known about him. The other six months, he works like a horse, leaving no time for Valeria. Before she got married, Valeria vehemently swore she would never follow in her mother's footsteps as the self-sacrificing wife. There was even a time when, deep down, she hated her mother's attitude, blaming her for her father's abandonment when they were children. But since her marriage, something clicked in her mind. She understood the role that everyone had played during that tragic October of 1993.

Valeria doesn't like to talk about it, but she knows that her marriage is more of a farce—a convenient arrangement for both her and her husband. Perhaps that's the case with all marriages, and those that aren't should not even exist. It was as obvious as declaring taxes for her husband. Still, she wouldn't torment her mother with such thoughts—the same woman who had always taught her that wives must endure their husbands, no matter how despicable they may be.

The two women meet in the house, exchanging looks that seem to search for something inexplicable in each other. The mother wants answers about Valeria's life, while the daughter silently conveys, "Don't get into my life; this is who I am, and I now have the capacity to decide for myself." Their lives have settled into an uncomfortable silence. Their gazes meet, and they opt to smile vaguely, for it is one of the few things they can do without irritating each other.

Monotony, frustration, and discord defined the relationship between Valeria and Mariela. It had been this way since one entered adolescence and the other aged, begrudgingly accepting the compromises life had imposed. To Valeria, her mother's "passivity" was unbearable. Every element of their shared history strained their bond—her father's abandonment, the natural rebellion of youth, stress, and the daughter's instinctive need to assign blame for the absence of the man they both had deeply loved. Valeria directed all her frustration at Mariela, transforming her into the darkest, most contemptible figure her mind could conjure.

Even before Valeria married, mysteries surrounded her parents' relationship and the motivations behind their conflicts. To her, her mother's passivity had been a significant factor, perhaps the root cause of her father's perpetual bad temper. She understood, on some level, that the couple's problems weren't entirely alien to her; they were "private matters" meant to stay within the walls of their bedroom. Yet, she saw her mother as childish, weak, stubborn, and preoccupied with trivialities. Her father, on the other hand, was far from a saint. Some issues were never kept secret, and among these were the most painful revelations for the family. Chief among them: her father's affair.

How many women there had been, Valeria couldn't say. But that wasn't the point. What tormented her for years was knowing her mother had been aware of the betrayal and had done nothing to preserve her dignity. Valeria couldn't forgive her for that, a resentment she carried openly for many years.

A single question haunted Valeria's mind: *Why did her mother stay with her father?* Even when his infidelity was blatant, even when everyone, including her, could see it? Why didn't she tell him the truth—that she deserved respect and not to be treated like a piece of furniture? In Valeria's eyes, her mother seemed a hollow shell of a woman. That's how she described her in her youth. But in time, Valeria came to realize that her mother now asked her the same question—about her own life. She fought desperately to avoid answering it, all the while haunted by the bitter irony that she had become just like her mother. This realization both enraged her and drove her mad in secret.

Valeria's life had never been simple. As the years passed, age became a relentless factor. One day, you're 25, in the prime of your youth; the next, you're 34, wondering where the years went, who stole them, and how it happened so quickly. Then, one day, a Lebanese man named Manzur entered her life. She married him, perhaps because during their courtship, he was all charm—handsome, intelligent, and affectionate. Although divorced with two children, he was the envy of all her friends, especially the few who remained single. Because, strangely, once someone marries, they seem to lose their single friends—as if some unspoken rule of marriage warns that a single woman might pose a threat to one's husband.

At first, things with Manzur were simple. He enjoyed traveling and taking Valeria everywhere, "showing her off" to his friends and colleagues, explaining the world through his perspective. But once he secured the papers to make her "his possession," life with him became an unbearable hell. Elías was a relentless womanizer, always using work as an excuse, just as Valeria's own father had done. Now, she knew firsthand what her mother had felt so many times.

Valeria was hopelessly in love with Elías and unwilling to leave him. At times, she rationalized his actions, telling herself he was working tirelessly to build a better financial future for them. She repeated this to herself endlessly, trying to believe it was true.

That morning, they exchanged only a few words. Valeria and her mother had little to say to one another. Deep down, Valeria felt guilty about the lack of communication between them, about the void that might never be filled again. She found it impossible to hold meaningful conversations with the woman who had brought her into the world. The guilt gnawed at her, yet it felt insurmountable. At that point, saying something like, *"I understand you now, Mom,"* would mean little. The conflicting emotions she harbored—resentment and affection toward her mother—were unbearable for them both.

The phone rang suddenly, its sharp, demanding tone shattering the silence, like an urgent, disoriented cry for attention. The sound jolted Valeria from her thoughts, clearing her mind. She reached for the receiver, but Mariela got there first, answering the call before Valeria could react.

Mariela listened in silence, her face betraying her struggle to process the words she was hearing. The seconds ticked by, each one stretching endlessly, as her expression shifted from confusion to sheer terror. She didn't say a word, but the look in her wide, plate-like eyes and the trembling corners of her mouth revealed the devastating message she had just received.

Suddenly, she dropped the cordless phone, her face twisted in an expression of unfiltered fear—the kind only terror can bring. A suffocating silence settled over the kitchen, deeper than before, broken only by the sharp sound of the phone hitting the floor and its plastic shell cracking on impact. That sound marked the end of a moment that would haunt both women for the rest of their lives.

Mariela stood frozen, seemingly trapped in another reality. Valeria, staring at her mother in shock and confusion, waited for an explanation. Finally, Mariela managed to speak, her voice choked and trembling, barely above a whisper.

"It's... your father. Your father... he's been kidnapped," she stammered through sobs, tears streaming down her face.

Without hesitation, Valeria wrapped her arms around her mother, holding her tightly while silently praying that this nightmare wasn't real.

Less than a minute later, Mariela's cell phone began to ring incessantly, its shrill tone filling the air. Valeria picked it up, assuming it was the kidnappers calling. But before answering, she checked the caller ID. It wasn't them. It was her brother, Fernando.

On the other end of the line, Fernando's familiar voice, unusually warm and steady, broke the tension for a fleeting moment. He told Valeria he had terrible news. She interrupted him, explaining that someone had already called the house, that their mother had answered and was now a sobbing wreck. Finally, she confirmed what they both feared—they knew their father had been kidnapped.

Turning on the television, they switched to the news channel. A special report was airing, with live footage from a helicopter showing the aftermath of the abduction of Raúl Pérez Brito.

Official Residence of Los Pinos, Mexico City, 12:54 PM, July 30th

The President of the Republic, Fidel Trevilla, prepared to deliver a message to the nation. This decision came just moments after answering the red phone in his office. A deep, impeccably articulate voice on the other end informed him:

- "Mr. President, something terrible has happened," the voice said, strained. "Senator Pérez Irigoyen's father has been kidnapped—right in the middle of Periférico just moments ago."

- "Impossible!" the President exclaimed in dismay. "Harlington is an incompetent fool!"

- "Mr. President, hundreds of thousands of citizens witnessed this tragic event unfold. We have advised the Ministry of the Interior to prepare a national broadcast."

- "And what exactly do you expect me to say to the public?" the President replied sarcastically. "That we don't know who took Pérez Irigoyen's father, but they should stay calm?" He paused. "I want details—answers."

- "Mr. President, with all due respect, we may be on the brink of an attack on the Mexican State. If you don't address the nation and emphasize the importance of resolving this incident, using the full force of the government to reassure citizens, we could face widespread panic." The voice paused, measured, then continued firmly. "Sir, Senator Pérez Irigoyen is regarded as one of the moral leaders of the opposition. It is critical to ensure the security of him and his family."

- "I don't need more pressure, Santibáñez. I know my government's responsibilities," Trevilla barked. "But I can't do this alone—you know what I mean. Convene an emergency security cabinet meeting immediately. And find Harlington—now. I need to speak to that clown."

The President hung up and leaned back, searching through his desk drawers until he found a stress ball. Squeezing it tightly, he reflected on how such a crisis could occur at the tail end of his administration. For years, the opposition had accused his government of enabling escalating violence and presiding over a failed state dominated by organized crime—claims he had always denied. But this incident changed everything.

For a moment, he considered the horrifying possibility: *What if they accused him of orchestrating the attack?* He buried his head in his hands, overwhelmed by the thought.

This was not the first time a politician's family member had been abducted. Five months earlier, Senator Fernández Cuéllar from Michoacán endured the kidnapping of her son. Two years ago, Congressman Juan Carlos Friechman of Chihuahua lost his brother to organized crime after weeks of negotiations ended in tragedy. What set this case apart was that Pérez Irigoyen wasn't just any politician—he was the moral compass of the opposition, a charismatic figure leading the polls for the presidency.

The President picked up his personal phone and scrolled through his contact list until he found Pérez Irigoyen's number. But he hesitated. Calling him informally could be misconstrued as collusion with criminal elements.

Instead, he consulted his spokesperson, seeking advice on whether to use an unsecured line to reach the senator. Both men, visibly anxious, deliberated for a moment. Finally, the President dialed.

- "Senator, this is the President of the United Mexican States," Trevilla said. "I'm reaching out regarding the events of this morning."

- "Mr. President, I deeply appreciate this gesture," Pérez Irigoyen responded with a composed tone. "As you know, my father is a patriot, just as you and I are."

- "Fernando, I assure you we will utilize every resource the State has at its disposal to find your father. Rest assured, everyone is working tirelessly on this." Trevilla paused briefly. "If you need anything, this is my personal number. Let me know immediately."

- "Mr. President, I..." Pérez Irigoyen's voice cracked with emotion. "I can only thank you. This means so much to me."

- "Senator, it's the least I can do," Trevilla replied. "As you said, we are patriots, committed to serving the nation's highest interests. I reaffirm my commitment to you, to national security, and to stability." He sighed audibly, his exhaustion evident. "We face challenging times. I must go now—I'm about to address the nation on this grave matter."

- "Thank you, Mr. President. I truly appreciate it."

The call ended. For a fleeting moment, the weight on Trevilla's shoulders seemed lighter. Just as he prepared to enter the press conference room, Alejandro Harlington, a rotund man in his early fifties, burst through the main door. He tried to speak, but Trevilla silenced him with a glare.

- "Alejandro, how does one '*lose*' the father of the most prominent opposition senator?"

- "Mr. President, with all due respect, he wasn't 'lost.' He was taken," Harlington stammered.

> - "'Taken,'" Trevilla repeated mockingly. "Alejandro, spare me the semantics. This is on you." He gestured toward the door leading to the press briefing area. "I don't want excuses—I want results. He's the opposition's moral leader, a man with industrial backing and close ties to telecommunications magnates. This incident could propel him as the de facto presidential candidate. We need to act swiftly, decisively, and flawlessly."

The President knows that now, more than ever, the conservatives need him. His duty as the head of the Executive Branch is to take decisive action, to be present, and to exercise leadership—qualities that are fundamental to his role. This situation, in a way, suits him perfectly because maintaining a civilized relationship with the opposition is part of the health of the democratic system. Senator Pérez is also gearing up for a significant campaign next year.

At that moment, twelve Interior Affairs advisors had already gathered. They had been meeting for over fifteen minutes, crafting a statement that had been approved by two deputy secretaries of the Interior, the Chief of Staff of the Presidency, and the Secretary of National Defense. Prior to the President's arrival at the location for the broadcast, two copy editors reviewed the statement, ensuring it met the standards for approval. The advisors also convened to finalize decisions related to the contingency plan for the search and rescue of Raúl Pérez.

The 65-second message was crafted around three central themes. The first emphasized the government's commitment to eradicating violence, its direct confrontation with organized crime, and reaffirmed the investment figures allocated by President Trevilla's administration to foster social order and peace. The second focused on reiterating the importance of cooperation between federal and state authorities, regardless of political affiliation or individual perspectives. Finally, the third underscored the strength of the country's institutional framework, assuring that there was no threat to the Mexican state or its people.

President Trevilla adjusted his tie and smoothed his suit as he prepared to face the camera. A makeup artist dabbed powder on his forehead and nose. The Presidential Radio and Television System countdown clock signaled 13 seconds to air. Across the country, commercials on every radio and TV station began to wrap up, synchronized for the message to commence at precisely 12:57 PM, Central Mexico Time. The commercials faded to a national broadcast banner reading: *"Message to the Nation from President Fidel Trevilla"* The floor manager began the countdown: five, four, three. Silently, he gestured two with his fingers, then one, and finally pointed at the President.

"Good afternoon, Mexicans. I address you today to inform you of the actions that the government I lead has decided to take in light of today's events. As you are aware, organized crime has launched a vile and cruel affront against the Mexican State, law enforcement, the rule of law, civility, and social peace. In their attempt to steal the tranquility of the Mexican nation, they have crossed a line. This is simply unacceptable, and now, more than ever, we must remain united and trust in the law.

As previously reported by the media, at noon Central Mexico Time, Mr. Raúl Pérez Brito—a businessman, patriot, exemplary citizen, and father of Senator Fernando Pérez Irigoyen, leader of the Acción Católica caucus—was abducted on the Periférico Sur in Mexico City. His whereabouts are currently unknown; however, emergency teams and federal forces are already on-site and working tirelessly.

The ballistic evidence gathered thus far provides us with reliable leads that will undoubtedly guide us to his location in the coming hours. We are confident that the perpetrators will be identified and swiftly brought to justice under federal jurisdiction. I commend the bravery of the emergency responders and law enforcement personnel from Mexico City and federal forces who have taken control of the situation and are closing in on those responsible.

Though this event constitutes an isolated incident, it will be pursued with the full weight of the law. The responsible party or parties will face exemplary punishment in strict adherence to legal due process.

The Government of Mexico stands in solidarity with the Pérez-Irigoyen family during these difficult times. Millions of voices across the nation join in calling for justice, peace, and respect for the rule of law as the cornerstone of a society that ensures opportunity for all. This is a moment to unite our efforts because only through unity can we become invincible."

The institutional music played, accompanied by a voiceover stating, ".*Government of Mexico, government of all*" A final banner closed the broadcast: *Message to the Nation from President Fidel" ".Trevilla*

As the transmission ended, the President noticed a slight tremor in his right hand and admitted to himself that he felt exhausted. A deep breath did little to alleviate the sweat pooling under his shirt and suit, and a mild heartburn crept into his digestive tract. He drank the glass of water behind him in one gulp before exiting the room.

In the improvised studio, the National Security Commissioner, Dr. Alejandro Harlington, entered quietly. Known for his slow gait and his preference for thick wool suits—even in the sweltering summer heat—Harlington exuded an aura of intrigue. He always carried an unlit cigarette between his lips, a habit he had been unable to break for years. It gave him the air of a private investigator from a Paco Ignacio Taibo II novel.

The President eyed him inquisitively, noting the Commissioner's advanced age. Everyone seemed older now than at the start of the administration. What had once been blond hair was now a crown of white atop Harlington's head, complemented by a bushy mustache of the same shade.

The president's message begins to cycle through on the teleprompter installed in front of Fidel Trevilla. For several minutes, the speech unfolds repetitively—word by word, paragraph by paragraph—until it exhausts itself. Harlington approaches Trevilla with his head slightly bowed, congratulating him on the message just delivered. He remarks that he agrees with the sentiment that law enforcement is doing an exceptional job. The president, however, struggles to keep his composure. He detests hearing people echo back what they think he wants to hear, yet he suppresses his frustration with considerable effort. A slight sheen of sweat forms on his brow, and the trembling in his right hand persists. Trevilla is visibly unnerved, breathing heavily and unable to fully regain his composure.

The situation has him deeply disturbed, even confused. Internally, he wrestles with the question of who could be the audacious scoundrel behind an attack so public that it lays bare his administration's ineptitude—surrounded, as he is, by a cadre of sycophants, incompetents, and fools.

Once free from the cameras' pressure, President Trevilla strides toward the National Security Commissioner, grips him by the shoulder, and speaks in a forceful tone:

- "Doctor, let me make myself perfectly clear: we cannot afford to become the laughingstock of this nation. Your so-called 'political career,' if we can even call it that, hangs by a thread. Whether it survives depends entirely on your ability to find a perpetrator in the next few hours." His eyes gleam with a fury that mirrors the fire coursing through his veins.

- "Mr. President, I understand," Alejandro Harlington replies in a calm tone. "I want you to know we're doing everything humanly possible to find answers."

- "Listen carefully, Alejandro," Trevilla snaps, slamming his hands against a nearby desk. "I'm not interested in speeches. I want answers, and I want them now! I don't care what the press says about you, the cabinet, or whether they blame organized crime. What matters to me is my reputation. This country is falling apart, and it's crushing us under its weight. Understand this, Harlington: this could destroy us."

Harlington remains silent. He isn't sure if there's an answer to give—or if one even exists. What he does know is that there were no prior warnings, no threats on record. Moments before arriving at Los Pinos, he had requested all triangulated phone data on the victim from the intelligence agency Cisen, but to his dismay, the information was scarce.

From the moment he was informed of the attack, Harlington had mobilized every resource to uncover even the faintest lead. His aides had immediately contacted the Ministry of the Interior and the

Ministry of National Defense. Yet, the information coming in was minimal. The Mexico City Public Security Secretariat had sent over just a handful of photographs, which Harlington carried in the inner pocket of his suit jacket. At one point, he tried to show them to the president, who dismissed him with a wave of his hand.

Witness accounts were contradictory. Some claimed they saw the black Lincoln lose control and crash into the median. Others reported a flash, like a gunshot, but differed on its origin—some swore it came from inside the campus of the technical institute, others from a nearby stationery store, while still others believed the shooter was positioned on a pedestrian bridge near a surveillance camera. The heavy rain made it impossible for anyone to give a clear description of the suspect.

The attack had occurred just an hour earlier, and ballistic tests were underway. Harlington had pressured the forensic team to deliver results as quickly as possible, knowing their careers depended on it. At the crime scene, the chaos was palpable: traffic snarled, police struggled to keep drivers from breaching the evidence perimeter, and forensic specialists in protective suits combed the area meticulously to avoid contaminating any potential clues. They had found around thirty spent cartridges near the scene. Inside the vehicle, Sergio's blood was everywhere, and his body lay slumped in the driver's seat, covered by a pale blue sheet. Despite their efforts, Harlington knew something had gone terribly wrong.

In his televised address, President Trevilla had emphasized the state's guarantee of public safety. Yet the truth was painfully clear: the Mexican state was faltering, vulnerable. Until a culprit was found, the president's authority and the justice system's legitimacy grew weaker with every passing moment. Harlington refrained from burdening the president with unnecessary details, limiting himself to a brief explanation that Cisen and SEDENA were already coordinating with the National Security Commission. Over seventy officers were scouring the crime scene, and a search was underway for the vehicle heading east toward the residence of Senator Pérez Irigoyen's father.

Trevilla listened, his expression a mix of disbelief and irritation. His breathing remained heavy and labored, resonating with the mounting pressure enveloping him.

"Look, Commissioner," the President began, his tone stern yet restrained, "in this job, your primary responsibility is to safeguard the political and public interests—mine, and those of the officials I designate—along with ensuring the population's safety. The media is on us like vultures. They're already demanding statements for the three o'clock news." He paused, raising his eyebrows for emphasis. "You know full well that I can't go out there and admit we have no idea where Mr. Raúl Pérez Brito is or explain the death of his companion without answers."

"Mr. President," the Commissioner responded, his voice tinged with genuine regret, "I assure you, give me two hours, and I will have firsthand information that will lead to the capture of the individual or individuals responsible for this 'unfortunate incident.'" His sincerity was palpable. "I have my best team working on it as we speak."

President Trevilla led the Commissioner and several security cabinet members—who had joined his impromptu march—into one of the boardrooms in the Presidential Office. Taking a deep breath, he resumed his exchange with Harlington. He laid out a series of directives with precision, starting with an unequivocal mandate: the matter was to be resolved within three days, or Harlington would be expected to submit his resignation without further prompting. "I trust that resignation will be on my desk without me needing to ask for it—because, frankly, I won't have the patience to even see you," the President added coldly.

Harlington inhaled deeply, nodding silently, before mumbling assurances that the matter would be resolved promptly. But the President wasn't finished. "Secondly," he continued, "I don't want a single statement to the press. Not a word. Nothing that could compromise the institutional image of this government or the presidency. Is that clear?" His gaze shifted to the other officials flanking the Commissioner. "This applies to all of you. Not one leak. My informants will let me know if anything slips, and I assure you, you'll regret it."

The Commissioner briefly held the President's gaze before cautiously raising some concerns about personnel and budget constraints. The President's eyes narrowed as he leaned in close, his voice dropping to a chilling whisper: "Commissioner, it seems you don't quite grasp the stakes of this situation. Let me make it simple: I want results, no matter the cost. I want him alive and in my custody within 72 hours. Do you understand, Alejandro?" His eyes seemed to bore into Harlington's soul as he finished. "Focus all your efforts—what little brainpower you and your team have—on overcoming the incompetence you've already demonstrated."

Taking a deep breath, the President licked his lips lightly and glanced at his watch before delivering the final blow: "I don't care if you have to resurrect the dead, drag guerrillas down from the mountains, or negotiate with enemies of the state. Bribe them, threaten them, or leverage their own shady deals—I don't care. Just find the idiot trying to make us look like absolute fools."

Harlington understood the unspoken directive: no stone was to be left unturned. He glanced at two of his subordinates, who promptly exited, while four others stepped forward, assuring him they would have actionable intelligence within two hours. The group dispersed swiftly, heading in different directions: east, north, and even into the historic city center, where they would pressure informants—threatening or rewarding as necessary.

Turning to his assistant, Harlington ordered him to keep him updated on every minute development. "Use the clearance we have. Talk to every informant, covert contact, and untouchable," he instructed. Though the assistant hesitated momentarily, he eventually handed Harlington a piece of paper filled with indecipherable scribbles. Harlington, familiar with the codes, tucked the note into his inner jacket pocket without a word.

Walking alone through the stark white corridors of the Presidential Residence, Harlington's mind raced. At the far end of the hallway was the President's office. Fidel Trevilla, the President, walked alongside him, glancing out a window that overlooked the residence grounds. Harlington noticed colleagues and other associates of the President arriving. He overheard Trevilla issuing orders to convene a "team"—likely the commission responsible for drafting a speech about Raúl Pérez Brito's death. From the corner of his eye, he saw Trevilla's contemptuous gaze and instinctively lowered his own, turning toward the exit.

Outside, helicopters and patrol cars swarmed the city. Harlington reflected bitterly on the futility of the city's vaunted surveillance system; despite its vast network, it had captured nothing useful. The one camera that might have provided a clue—located on the south wing of the Mexico City Tech campus—had been vandalized and was out of service. He stared at the lifeless plastic casing with its opaque black lens and retrieved seven photographs from his jacket pocket. These were all they had: images from four days earlier, the last ones stored on the camera's damaged hard drive.

The photos showed two individuals: one, a man in his forties with cropped hair, thick glasses, and a garish salmon-colored shirt; the other, a heavyset man with a perpetual scowl, his furrowed brow marked by deep vertical lines. Though they appeared in four of the seven photos, they provided no definitive lead. The Commissioner traced their faces with his finger, considering whether to send the images to an AI biometric lab. Yet he hesitated—any success would mean the credit would go to the intelligence agency rather than his own team. And failure? That would waste precious time.

Climbing into a Suburban headed for his office on Constituyentes Avenue, Harlington felt a nagging unease. Something told him his current approach wasn't enough. Abruptly, he changed course. Instead of returning to his office, he instructed the driver to take him to the crime scene. There, he would personally oversee the forensic team, determined to uncover what his subordinates might have missed.

Safe House, Sierra de Santa Catarina, Mexico City; 12:42 PM, July 30th.

Tinaco and I arrived at the agreed meeting point. Our contact was waiting for us, explaining that we'd need to "lend a hand." It wasn't unusual for us to be asked for favors; after all, this is what makes us professionals in the kidnapping business. These requests could vary widely in nature. Our new task was to keep an eye on the old man for a few hours until we got the boss's call. In this line of work, there are never precise hours, but that's just how it is. This is how we've made a living our entire lives.

We dragged over some rickety chairs while a scrawny kid, who we soon learned went by the name "Chucho," began tying up the victim. Tinaco scolded him repeatedly for his sloppy knots, which were too loose to hold the man securely. After several attempts, the boy finally managed to restrain the old man. He subdued him by pressing a knee against his back and pulling the man's arms so tightly that it pushed the limits of human endurance. The old man let out a low groan, only to receive a hard punch to his left ear in return.

Tinaco stepped in, firmly grabbing the victim and seating him on a chair, where he finished the job, securing the remaining knots to immobilize him completely. Chucho watched Tinaco with wide-eyed admiration, acknowledging his skill in what he called "the business." Somewhere beneath Tinaco's hardened exterior, his heart swelled with pride. He knew the boy looked up to him and would likely do so for the rest of his life. Secretly, Tinaco felt good about mentoring him.

Once the old man was gagged to keep him from making noise, they returned to the couch where I sat. I was exhausted, trembling slightly, my mouth parched. I couldn't even muster the energy to fetch a glass of water. A strange heaviness had settled over me. My breathing was uneven, and fatigue weighed me down. My eyes were fixed on some random point in the grease-streaked, grimy room. The white floor, littered with beige stones, was encrusted with filth, the kind that comes from years of neglect.

I peeled off my damp black gloves, sticky from the humidity and the long hours I'd spent hiding under the pedestrian bridge. My hands trembled slightly as I examined them, as if searching for answers in my fingers or palms. Removing the tape from my middle and ring fingers, I tossed the sticky mess onto the floor and collapsed back into the couch.

After a moment, I asked the boy his age. "Thirteen," he replied curtly, barely acknowledging me. His dismissive tone didn't escape Tinaco, who reprimanded him harshly: "Show some respect for the man. That's *El Pasa*! He's back in the business, and you're just a snot-nosed kid who knows nothing about all this man has accomplished in his life. Ask your father, ask your uncles who *El Pasa* is. They'll tell you about the loads of goods he trafficked and the men he killed back when he was your age."

Your age. That last phrase echoed in my mind, as if planting a seed of doubt that took root in the center of my brain. I stared into the void, my thoughts distant, while the boy stammered out an apology to me and *Tinaco*. As they continued their exchange, I drifted into a parallel reality, remembering how I'd begun my own criminal career—unknowingly, without even recognizing it as something bad until much later.

I muttered to *Tinaco* that it didn't matter, that memories fade into oblivion and that none of it was important. The truth was, I was deeply unsettled by being there. For a moment, I couldn't even remember why I was at this safe house. Why had I just shot a man I'd never met on the Periférico? Why had I kidnapped an old man? Why had our informant been so accurate about our target?

Now, here I was, waiting—for what, I didn't know. Waiting where, I couldn't say. And so I sat still and silent.

Tepito Neighborhood, Mexico City. Years Ago.

As I sat there once more, motionless and silent, my eyes fixed on my trembling hands and the pale whiteness under my fingernails, a memory surfaced. I was six years old, and my dream was to become a police officer. Whenever I announced it in public, people would give me odd looks. Back then, I thought we needed more officers—a noble profession, full of respect and social honor. Although I didn't really understand what those things meant, I believed that wearing a blue uniform was the right way to live. Now, looking back, I realize I used to think life was a game and that the world was neatly divided into good and bad.

What I didn't know was that my father, along with my entire family, had always been thieves—any kind of thieves—likely since the dawn of time. There was a peculiar sense of pride in this legacy. As I grew older, it became clear that my ideas had been shaped entirely by my mother's judgment. From those early days until I turned twelve, my memories are sparse, almost nonexistent. Only faint, scattered images occasionally come to mind. By the time I reached twelve, my mother had passed away, and my father, consumed by drugs and other vices like gambling, had abandoned us. All he left behind was his family—a brother, who in turn had me.

At fourteen, I remember having stolen nearly 1,800 side mirrors, taillights, bumpers, grilles, and even entire sets of tires. Looking back now, it strikes me how quickly one evolves in this business. The path takes you without you realizing it. It's hard to pinpoint when or how you start because the beginning always feels innocuous. Stealing to eat is the lowest form of existence for a human being, but it becomes normalized through sheer survival. In my case, I think it was at fourteen that it truly began, although perhaps that's just an easy way to justify myself. Sometimes, I think this isn't even my story—it's the story of everyone born into a generation steeped in violence and fear.

It's hard for me to reconcile that I was part of that story, now so distant and blurred. The memories come with a haze, making it impossible to see everything clearly. A veil of nostalgia seems to drape over every image my mind manages to summon. And yet, there's an odd tenderness in remembering that young boy who once roamed the streets, who, with a group of delinquents, terrorized the dimly lit avenues of the Morelos district. Back then, the sodium-vapor streetlights gave the night a faint yellow hue—a sickly light we used to blend into as we stripped strangers of their belongings, targeting anyone we deemed an outsider, a foreigner, or someone from another neighborhood.

Starting is always easy. You don't even realize you're heading toward something uncertain. Perhaps it's because the beginning is inevitably fun. It starts with a simple side mirror—ripping it off and running away. Your heart races as your legs propel you forward. It feels like flying without wings—that's the thrill of being "initiated" into the art of delinquency.

Once you're deeper into it, you realize, at least superficially, what you've done—that you've grown and can sustain yourself. But soon, society's expectations push you toward bigger thrills and, especially, more money. And, no matter how frowned upon, the only way you know to get it is by stealing. One day, during a robbery, you stumble upon a gun. My first gun didn't even work, but no one else knew that. You show it off, carry it everywhere, and that's how you start threatening people—clueless bystanders, pedestrians, bus riders. Sometimes you smack them on the head with the butt of the gun. Other times, you settle for the sheer terror etched on their faces when they see your weapon. Perhaps that's what feeds your drive—the respect you gain that you've never had before.

When I turned fifteen, I got that broken gun from a "compa" who had already been to prison twice. I traded it for a Volkswagen Atlantic grille, a pair of headlights, and a spoiler—all stolen from the Buenos

Aires neighborhood. By then, I had become proficient at dismantling parts in seconds. I accepted the gun with pride, understanding that it symbolized something greater. It marked my transition into adulthood and my initiation into the world of crime. It earned me money, elevated my status among my crew, and even came with perks—like a girlfriend who, of course, didn't stick around long.

I knew very little about firearms. I'd seen them but had never paid close attention—not the kind of attention you give when you want to understand something completely. Looking back, I think I was incredibly distracted during my teenage years.

It was during that time, when I was just starting out in this line of work, that something happened I still can't fully explain to this day. One night, while attempting to rob a few pedestrians, they somehow realized my weapon wasn't functional—a fact I had assumed only I knew. Those I meant to strip of their belongings turned on me, chasing me down several blocks. Luckily, I managed to escape, though not without suffering some punches, kicks, and scrapes. Perhaps that was the most harrowing experience I endured in this trade, which is why I still recall it with bitter resentment.

Several blocks later, with my heart pounding in my chest and a buzzing in my head, I hid for what felt like an eternity in the doorway of a tenement. I stayed there until I felt sure the danger had passed. I remember slinking back to my dwelling, where I barricaded myself for three full days and nights, unwilling to step outside. Maybe something inside me had broken.

After those days of seclusion, I recounted the ordeal to one of my contacts at the time—a skinny man with a bony face and a frail frame, especially in his hands and legs. He was extremely tall and a bit slow-witted. People called him "El Gorrión" (The Sparrow). After laughing heartily at my misfortune and mocking my ineptitude as a "crook," he remarked how absurd it was for a would-be thief to end up "robbed." I explained that it couldn't have turned out any other way, as my revolver was nonfunctional. Though I'd thought no one else knew, perhaps a snitch had gotten word of my insignificant calamity, and by now, the whole neighborhood likely knew of my humiliation.

El Gorrión offered to get me a real gun, one that worked and would safeguard my reputation. He assured me it wouldn't fail in future stick-ups. What's more, for the first time, I'd have the ability to take a life in exchange for someone's belongings. I agreed without hesitation. Deep down, it felt like the realization of all my dreams up to that point. A wave of exhilaration swept over me and stayed for days and weeks. Some peculiar sense of satisfaction coursed through my veins, making me feel alive, important, respected, and ready to accomplish something great.

It took three long weeks for the delivery to reach me, but when El Gorrión finally arrived with it, wrapped in a coarse paper bag, and placed it in my hands, I felt the heft of the pistol. A profound sense of power and invincible security filled me. When I finally loaded it, I saw the glory ahead of me. No longer would I bluff with a useless, unloaded weapon; now, I had the power of life and death at my fingertips.

I remember acquiring a box of .22 caliber bullets for my new gun. It was a small weapon, but far heavier than the first, likely because this one was fully operational. I passed my old revolver down to one of my friends in the neighborhood. He was the boldest in acts of vandalism and had always looked up to me for my actions. His name was Ramiro, though I haven't heard from him in ages. I recall the look on his face when he received my gift. I instructed him to use it wisely and explained that I'd removed part of the firing mechanism so he wouldn't pose a threat to me. Still, it would suffice to intimidate anyone he wished to rob.

With the new gun in my possession, I must admit, I spent countless nights familiarizing myself with its components. It was almost impossible to reassemble it at first, but I dedicated entire days to cleaning and examining it—the barrel, the trigger, the magazine, the safety, the chamber, and the firing pin. It became my obsession. I practiced loading it quickly, envisioning situations where I might have to return fire against the police or the military. I rehearsed ejecting a bullet and catching it mid-air, and I perfected my aim. Yet I never fired it. A certain fear overcame me every time I tried.

Day and night, I kept the gun close. It was always within reach, even while I slept. I'd place it under my makeshift pillow, feeling the cold metal press against my ear. Back then, my brother and I lived in a shack filled with sugarcane presses. Sometimes, in the dead of night, we'd wake startled by distant gunfire or the wailing of police sirens. Still, there was something, as I recall, that always made us happy—perhaps a false memory, but one I choose to preserve. They were the moments we shared in that shack, a place we once dared to call home.

I didn't pull the trigger on anyone—not until months after I acquired it. One morning in March, two of my closest friends came to tell me that my brother had been found dead in the student plaza. He'd been shot twice—once in the head and once in the leg. That was the saddest day of my life, even more so than when my mother passed or when our father disappeared forever. That night, grief and anxiety consumed me. Not even holding the gun could bring me comfort.

Despair had me in its grip, for I'd never imagined losing the only family I had left. You always think you'll have time, that you'll grow old together. My brother and I used to dream of change during those long, hungry nights. We'd promise each other things would get better. We'd go north, like our father did, earn seven dollars an hour, buy a house, marry an American woman, and eat McDonald's every day. But that day, there he was—lifeless before me. There was nothing I could do. It felt as if time itself had betrayed me, leaving me powerless to undo his stillness.

I became consumed by a single thought: to kill anyone involved in my brother's death. As his body lay on a cold metal slab, I swore to myself in secret that this vow would become the sole driving force of my existence. Later, when they handed him over to me, I was at a loss for what to do. A kind-hearted woman, a true Samaritan, helped me gather the money needed for the coroner to issue the death certificate. People from the neighborhood accompanied me while the Medical Examiner's Office deigned to release his body. Back at the place we called home, I approached him and silently promised that I would avenge his murder. I made this pledge by his makeshift coffin—a cardboard box, the only thing I could afford that day.

I still remember the grief that overwhelmed me, a sorrow so profound it felt like being consumed by a serpent devouring itself. But that was a pain only I could feel, because no one else could understand the depth of my loss. On that day, it wasn't just my brother who died; a part of me perished with him.

I cried for so long that I ran dry, my body emptied of tears and my heart rotting away. For three days and nights, I lay motionless in a dilapidated armchair, rocking back and forth, clutching a weapon in my hands. In that oppressive silence, I thought only of my brother's lifeless face, replaying his smile in my memory, and asking myself who could have killed him with such cruelty.

The neighbors took care of his remains. They buried him in an old grave at the Dolores Cemetery, one that a kind neighbor gave us. Most people knew my mother had passed away and my father had abandoned us for the United States long ago. While some genuinely sympathized with me, others feigned compassion, muttering mockery and contempt behind my back. Were it not for the solidarity of the neighbors, I can't imagine what would have become of us. People from the bottom of society have a unique kind of solidarity, a moral commitment to look after one another, to show care and respect—most of the time.

In those days, I lost all faith. I stopped crossing myself at the street altars, their meaning drained of significance. Divinity dissolved from my consciousness, and the saints and virgins I once revered became hollow images. For a long while, I couldn't even recall my brother's funeral, though I knew I must have been there. It was as if my mind had erased that day from existence. Instead, I remembered the rosary prayers held for him, in one of the historic center's churches, far from home. Some people suspected, not without reason, that whoever had killed my brother might also come for me.

I, for my part, put my faith only in my weapon and its bullets. I constantly told myself this was the only justice I needed. Armed, I entered the church, my fingers brushing the cold steel under my clothes. That icy sensation was the thread keeping me, in my mind, sane. Deep down, I wanted someone to confront me, to call my name and draw their gun, so we could settle everything with bullets. But nothing happened.

It took many sleepless nights before I tracked down the first culprits. In the barrio, nothing stays hidden for long; rumors travel fast. I began working more intensely—not just stealing car parts or robbing buses. I started targeting wealthier neighborhoods for watches and distributing contraband, from drugs to stolen goods. I even took part in highway heists and once raided a train in Ecatepec. All of this was for one purpose: to buy information about those responsible for my brother's death.

I interrogated drifters and addicts in the plaza. Some offered nonsense, others' stories aligned, but just when I thought I was uncovering the truth, my informants would vanish—or worse, turn up dead. It felt like the truth was always just out of reach, like a house of cards collapsing with the slightest breeze. At times, it seemed everyone but me knew what had happened.

In my darkest moments, I sought to dull the pain by cutting my arms and hands. The scars remain as silent witnesses to that anguish. The suffering stretched on for months. Compassionate souls didn't lack; neighbors fed me and worried over my sleeplessness. Some urged me to let my brother rest in peace, to stop chasing something only God and the saints could unravel. Others tried to pull me out of this wretched life, but no one succeeded in changing my resolve.

Perhaps they couldn't grasp what he meant to me. He was all I had. That rainy, gray afternoon, when barely half a dozen people attended his burial, I watched his remains lowered into the ground. For the last time, I swore vengeance.

Time passed, my mind weakened, and my memories blurred. But one thing became clear: about ten months after his death, I heard of a gang in the barrio clashing with another. Their leader, they said, went by the nickname "El Gato." Multiple sources pointed to him as my brother's killer. For the first time, I saw him from a distance. I didn't care about his motives; I only knew he had taken the most precious thing I had.

For weeks, I tracked his movements, fully convinced of his guilt. In our barrio, three fingers pointing at you are enough to confirm your culpability. I focused all my energy on this task, letting my life revolve around it. I learned he always carried a gold-plated pistol engraved with the figure of Santa Muerte. His gang treated him like a god, willing to die for him. This made my job harder.

I observed that he never missed a lucha libre event at the Arena Coliseo. He went without his usual entourage, accompanied only by his girlfriend. Scanning the wrestling schedule, I found three key matches featuring his favorite wrestler, Fray Infierno. These were my opportunities to strike.

Selling stolen goods and working through sleepless nights, I scraped together enough to attend all three matches. I bribed the arena guards to smuggle in a knife alongside my gun, planning for a swift, quiet kill. My hope was to catch him unguarded, perhaps in the bathroom, and leave him to bleed out before disappearing into the crowd.

But the first match didn't go as planned. He never left his seat, engrossed in the spectacle of Fray Infierno's acrobatics. Still, I knew my chance would come. This wasn't over.

There, I observed several phenomena. The first was that "El Gato" indeed attended the event alone, without any members of his gang. He genuinely enjoyed the spectacle, to the point of losing himself in the acrobatic ballet performed masterfully by men averaging 230 kilos, launching themselves from the top rope only to crash onto a prone body on the mat. I focused on every expression and gesture the despicable murderer made. His enjoyment, reflected in his wide smile, filled me with disgust. I felt nauseated watching him cheer and shout with excitement. Yet, I realized that those emotions seemed to absorb him completely, relaxing his awareness of his surroundings. Those acrobatics appeared to be a kind of drug, lulling him into a stupor that prevented him from being fully present.

Throughout the match, I studied every scream, gesture, and expression he made from his seat. I noticed that he had a woman on his lap, someone who must have been about my age. During the entire performance, which lasted quite a while, she never once received his attention—not even by accident. He busied himself touching her legs and buttocks, occasionally running his hand along her stomach or slipping it beneath her blouse, all while shouting enthusiastically and cursing whenever something in the rhythmic choreography struck him as unfair or disadvantageous to his favorite wrestler, “Fray Infierno.” I didn't understand the rules of these oversized acrobats' grappling matches, but for a brief moment, I entertained a foolish fantasy: imagining myself in the ring, facing "El Gato." In my mind, the match ended in my triumph. But as I snapped back to reality, I noticed that when the event ended, he left quickly. I hurried to follow him, but the crowd made it impossible. That was when I realized I needed to sit closer to him next time. Sitting too far away and waiting until the end of the show was a mistake—everyone rushed to leave at once.

On my second visit to the wrestling arena, I focused on observing the outside environment. While I knew there was security, the place was essentially gang territory. They controlled everything—from drug sales to prostitution and the informal food vendors, who paid "protection fees" to the dominant gang. Those selling clothing or other goods had to hand over a portion of their merchandise to the leaders. There were no issues with the police; the local gangs paid them off, securing their protection and leniency. As I strategized, I began to think it might be better to kill him at the start of the event. Yet, I kept revising this thought, reasoning it might be safer to act at the end. On that day, I arrived early at the arena. I knew it was the second-to-last night I could be certain "El Gato" would be there. I studied the dim, gray streets and identified the alley beside the building where he would enter. It was filled with restaurant garbage: crates piled high with food scraps, swarms of flies buzzing over them, and an unpleasant stench—a mix of sewage and rotting food.

That day, a homeless man had taken up residence amid the trash piles. I approached him and asked:

- "Hey, mate, do you happen to know a guy they call 'El Gato?'" I asked, without much effort to hide my intent.

- "Everyone knows 'El Gato.' He's a damn showoff," he replied, clutching a small flask as if I might try to snatch it away.

- "He always comes here to watch the matches, right?" I added, handing him ten Sor Juana coins.

- "Yeah, he's all talk," he said, extending his hand to take the coins. "His favorite wrestler is 'Fray Infierno,' the one who rigs the matches."

- "So, he always exits through this door?" I probed.

- "Yeah, but no big deal. He's just a lousy punk," I lied.

- "Yeah, a lousy punk," the man mumbled before closing his eyes and retreating into his stupor.

I thought that would be the day—the moment to act. But something told me it wasn't the right time. My hands trembled, and a ringing began in my ears. Once inside the arena, sweat dripped down my back, and I realized I didn't have the courage yet. Again, I watched "El Gato" cheer and lose himself in excitement. This time, he was with another woman, yet he followed the same routine: touching her casually, ignoring her entirely otherwise.

A crucial thought struck me during this second encounter: I had never killed anyone before. That fact alone made using a firearm to end his life seem implausible. The enormity of such an act paralyzed me. On top of that, I wasn't confident I could get close enough to make him my target. He never got up—not even to use the bathroom—and remained glued to his seat. Even if an opportunity arose, "El Gato" was a much taller, stronger man than I was.

During that fight, the crowd erupted with every hold, every pinfall attempt as backs were pressed flat against the canvas of the ring. The referee, a man named Tropicasas, would drop to the mat alongside the wrestlers, closely inspecting whether a shoulder had indeed touched the canvas. His count, from one to three, was punctuated by thunderous slaps against the mat, sparking roars from the audience. Fans either cheered wildly or jeered in disdain, depending on their allegiance to the classic factions of lucha libre: técnicos or rudos.

Meanwhile, I couldn't stop thinking about how to kill the brute who watched the acrobatics of these people's heroes with such indifference. For ten nights following that match, I mentally reviewed every move performed by El Gato. I could recall every expression on his face, every gesture, and even the frustration he showed whenever Fray Infierno was overpowered by other fighters. The theory was all there, but putting it into practice proved far more challenging than I had initially thought.

In the mornings, I would head to an empty lot, armed with soda and beer cans as targets. I practiced my aim relentlessly, gradually mastering the recoil of the weapon. At first, the kickback would throw me off balance, but with time, I improved significantly, hitting the cans with increasing accuracy. Still, shooting at lifeless, stationary objects was nothing like facing a living, breathing being—something that moved, ran, and could even fight back.

Beyond the technical challenge, there was a psychological and emotional barrier to overcome. If I chose to shoot, I'd only have one chance. One bullet had to hit a vital spot. If it didn't kill him, I'd have to flee the scene and leave the city. Failing to escape would mean only one thing: a trip straight to hell.

In the days leading up to the main event—the night El Gato would meet his end—I upped the ante in my training. I brought two old dogs to that vacant lot, and, for the final test, a cat. The cat managed to escape, leaving no trace behind, though perhaps the dogs had made a meal of it. I couldn't be sure, as I found no bones or tufts of fur. The dogs, on the other hand, served their purpose: they helped me conquer the fear of killing something that breathed.

Those poor creatures were already knocking on death's door before my bullets pierced them. It wasn't easy, but I forced myself to keep my sights steady, my hands unwavering. The flash from the barrel briefly blinded me each time I fired, delaying my view of the bullet's outcome. Even so, I couldn't be certain this practice was enough. Yet, my rage and the vow of vengeance I'd made to my brother felt like sufficient fuel to see it through.

The night before the event, I said goodbye to the miserable shack that had borne witness to my misfortunes. In gratitude, I gifted my neighbors the statue of the saint dressed in a green robe—the one my family and I had been so devoted to. They placed it in an empty niche in the courtyard, where it stood like a silent sentinel.

As for my belongings, I left my meager wardrobe—a few clothes in pistachio-green crates—to my gang. They could wear or sell them as they wished, and they thanked me profusely. Some begged me not to leave, urging me to stay and keep working with them, swearing we'd soon rise to the top in "the business." We consoled one another.

To those who had taken care of my brother's remains, I gave the few pieces of furniture we owned, including the stove—the most valuable item in our possession. The photos of my family and me, however, I burned myself.

Word spread quickly through the neighborhood that I was leaving. Many came to bid me farewell. I stuck to my story: I was heading to Puebla, which was a lie, but not a random one. I didn't want anyone to know my true destination, especially since I didn't know it myself. All I knew was that I couldn't go to Puebla.

That afternoon, I dressed entirely in black—not just because the event would be at night, but because it would allow me to blend into the shadows. If necessary, I could climb rooftops and slip away from the police or El Gato's gang under the dim, yellowish streetlights of the city. The second reason for wearing black was practical: blood was less noticeable on dark clothing.

I left home knowing I would never return. My right pocket held all the money I had, while the gun rested at my waist, hidden under a black hoodie. In my left pocket, I carried an ice pick. My medallion of Saint Jude, which had accompanied me since birth, I left behind on the windowsill for someone with more faith than me to find.

I walked out of the tenement and gave one last goodbye to Doña Panchita, an old woman who had always shown me kindness. I kissed her forehead and told her I was leaving. She blessed me and assured me that whatever I was about to do, it would ultimately be for the best. I simply nodded.

And with that, I stepped into the night.

I walked under the rain, careful to avoid meeting the eyes of anyone who might recognize me. Each step I took left a footprint that was quickly erased by the gentle water pouring from the sky, flooding the pavement once more. When I reached the narrow street, packed with vehicles and a throng of people shouting, shoving, and crowding the entrance, the security team at the Arena struggled to contain the human tide. Yet, I joined the access line, clutching my ticket in one hand while my hopes tightened in my chest.

At the checkpoint, I handed over five bills featuring Lázaro Cárdenas to the guard ensuring no weapons entered. With a knowing nod, he allowed me through into the Arena, which tonight seemed unlike anything I had seen before. I found my seat, feeling as if I were floating in the clouds—a strange sensation. My hands were clammy, my mouth dry, and a knot tightened in my throat. At the same time, I had the urge to stand in the center of the ring and scream with all my might until I collapsed, breathless, purging the unbearable pain in my soul. Yet outwardly, I remained calm, unnervingly composed. I sipped a beer, trying to steady myself, unsure if it was the alcohol or the sight of my target, *El Gato*, that finally brought me peace. The moment he entered, I could breathe again, focusing solely on him—his gestures, his movements—anticipating his downfall.

This was the moment of truth, my chance to prove I was worthy of vengeance. I told myself I was. This was my opportunity to earn a name, not just in my neighborhood but everywhere I went. After tonight, *El Pasa* would be the most feared man wherever he settled. But this wasn't just about a name; it was about weapons, maturity, keeping my word to my family—it was a matter of honor.

With every slam of a wrestler's back against the canvas, with every booming announcement from the commentator, something deep within me stirred violently. It jolted me, made me shiver. I didn't know if everyone else felt the same, but I was painfully aware of my actions and their consequences. My mind wandered to what might become of my soul. Hell was the only option now. If *El Gato's* crew caught me, they'd kill me at the very least. If the police showed up, I'd have no choice but to end it myself. I ignored the match entirely, only tuning in as the end approached.

When the referee Tropicasas counted to three, the crowd erupted in unison, chanting the winner's name. Soon, they would carry him out on their shoulders, hailing him as the greatest gladiator in Arena history. For these fans, his world was contained within a four-by-four-meter ring. By then, I was just two rows away from my brother's killer. My blood boiled, my heart pounded, but I focused, fixed on his wretched existence.

The masked wrestler exited on the shoulders of adoring fans, bathed in the glare of spotlights and flashes from cameras. As they celebrated, I saw *El Gato* slipping toward the locker room area. I knew he would exit through the side door. My focus sharpened; there was no tomorrow for me. I saw him weaving through the crowd, heading for the door. Before reaching it, he exchanged a few words with Fray Infierno, the night's champion, and held hands with a woman—another one, different from any of the others I'd seen him with. I pushed through the distracted crowd, quickening my pace, and exited through the main door. I ran to the alleyway, gripping my revolver tightly, teeth clenched like someone bracing for an inevitable collision with something solid.

I sprinted along the side of the Arena, just as the alley door began to open. I ran faster, positioning myself before it could swing fully. Something made *El Gato* and his companion hesitate and try to retreat into the building. I slammed the heavy metal door shut. In the dim light, I saw two figures. The man's arm wrapped around the woman's waist, just steps ahead of me. I banged the door shut and shouted, "*Gato!*"

He turned, responding with words I couldn't understand. I drew my gun and, with all the strength in my body, fired twice. I can still remember the sparks, the heat in my hands, and the strange tingling sensation that comes after shooting another human being. His silhouette crumpled to his knees as his companion screamed. The impulse to drop the weapon and run nearly overtook me, but her pleas to spare her life stopped me. I decided she could be useful, the sole witness to the act. She became my hostage as we walked out of the alley to the main street, where the chants and hysteria over a hero's victory drowned out the gunshots and the death of a tyrant.

We flagged down a taxi, and once far enough away, I let her go. I left and vowed never to return to this furious, chaotic city. That's how it all began, how I started down this path.

The sound of rain pulls me out of my reverie as Tinaco's voice reminds me that our replacements aren't coming anytime soon—the rain delays everything.

July 30th, 2:35 PM. Periférico Sur, Mexico City—Scene of the Kidnapping

The Senator stood leaning against a tree, a cigarette burning slowly between his fingers—not by his own doing, but by the relentless wind that consumed it. Fernando had never smoked before, nor had he ever felt such an overwhelming sense of emptiness, fear, and uncertainty. Exhaustion had taken him captive, and the light drizzle, mildly annoying, continued to fall on his disheveled figure. His weary, hollow-eyed demeanor mirrored the cigarette, gradually vanishing as it burned between his long index and middle fingers.

His gaze was lost in the endless horizon of mountains and ridges. Seconds dragged into minutes as his watch ticked on, marking over forty minutes of anxious waiting for any news to ease the crushing stress of uncertainty. Below, the scene resembled an anthill. Countless cars clogged the roads, their drivers craning their necks to catch glimpses of the scene: forensic teams photographing in every direction, marking bullet casings on the asphalt with crude chalk circles. Swarms of officers and agents redirected traffic on the nation's most important avenue, creating a staggering nine-kilometer jam.

Each drag of his cigarette seemed to suffocate something within him. The smoke he exhaled carried his faint hope, dissipating into the atmosphere, swept away by the wind. The passing minutes brought no clarity, leaving Fernando—who always had answers—adrift in confusion. Suddenly, the voice of a man snapped him back to the present. It was Pablo Gordillo, the Attorney General, coordinating the data collection efforts. Gordillo, a retired military officer in his mid-fifties, had piercing black eyes and a perpetually unwell demeanor.

Gordillo relayed the President's concerns, which had been communicated to him and Alejandro Harlington, who had personally met with the President due to the sensitive nature of the situation.

Fernando thanked Gordillo sincerely for his attention and updates. The former soldier informed him that they were nearly ready to recover the body that the Senator had already identified as his father's driver and bodyguard. A black vehicle appeared among the official cars, carrying Fernando's mother and sister.

His relationship with his sister had been strained for years—three, to be precise. They hadn't spoken, perhaps due to Fernando's relentless work schedule or misplaced priorities, always assuming there'd be enough time to make up for missed family dinners and postponed gatherings. But there was no time for words now—only a silent embrace and shared tears, stifled sobs drowned in their grief.

The Attorney General kept his distance, allowing the family a moment to express their pain and frustration. Fernando's mother recounted the chilling phone call she had received from the captor—a voice cold and devoid of humanity, speaking in a monotone gray that matched the bleakness of the day. Gordillo assured them that his best agents were tracing the call and had dispatched specialized equipment recently procured from Israel to the Senator's parents' residence.

"We'll establish the rescue operations center in a strategic location for optimal coordination," Gordillo explained to the family. Fernando expressed his gratitude and requested a moment alone with his mother and sister.

Just then, Gordillo received a call from one of his most trusted operatives. The agent reported they had located a person of interest who was now en route to the central headquarters on Avenida Paseo de la Reforma. The informant insisted that the individual would cooperate only under specific conditions. Gordillo, holding his menthol cigarette with his shoulder and ear, listened carefully. After a brief pause, the voice on the line resumed, its tone cautious and urgent.

Gordillo flicked the cigarette butt into a grassy area by the Periférico and asked whether Commander Alejandro Harlington had been informed. The agent confirmed, though he expressed reservations about the commander's proposed course of action. Gordillo, however, chose to disregard the operative's doubts—crisis moments were no time to question subordinates' opinions.

He ended the call, issued field instructions, and prepared to leave just as the Mexico City Mayor's helicopter touched down at the nearby nutrition hospital. Secretly, Gordillo dreaded encountering the Mayor at that moment. Administrative disagreements had soured their relationship, and he had no desire to face the man, whom he viewed as an ambitious politician already posturing for the presidency. Deciding to act swiftly, Gordillo approached Fernando, handed him a business card with his private number, and excused himself.

As Gordillo's team departed for their headquarters on Reforma, the cacophony of the helicopter masked their retreat. Meanwhile, the Senator was approached by the Mayor and his security team. They assured him of their unwavering commitment to finding his father and pledged close collaboration with federal authorities. Such assurances were hardly surprising; Manuel Vela Márquez, the Mayor, had been Fernando's classmate in law school. Their friendship, though rare among career politicians, had endured despite belonging to opposing political factions.

Manuel Vela knew this would be a complicated and grueling afternoon—the kind that any politician dreads. He approached the tree that now served as his friend's makeshift office. Holding a cigarette between his fingers, he fixed his gaze on Fernando's eyes. They looked distant, burdened by devastation. Manuel placed a hand on his shoulder and, leaning in, said:

- "Fernando, I understand what you're going through. No one would want to be in your shoes."

- "I never imagined it would be like this, Manuel," the Senator replied sincerely. "I don't know if I can handle this much pressure."

- "You have no choice but to endure it. You must, for them," Manuel said, gesturing toward Fernando's mother and sister, who were waiting in a vehicle nearby. "You can't give up. We'll support you in every way we can. I know it's our responsibility, but according to intelligence reports, no one had any prior knowledge. It's as if ghosts were behind this."

- "Ghosts," Pérez Irigoyen echoed, staring into the distance. "It wasn't supposed to happen like this, Manuel."

- "We'll get through this. It will strengthen you—not politically, but as a person. Sometimes, things like this remind us that we're just human beings. You must stay strong. Let me take you and your family out for a meal," Manuel suggested, pausing to meet Fernando's eyes again. "I know you want to stay here until there's news, but punishing yourself like this won't help."

- "Thank you, Manuel, but I don't want to be around anyone right now. I need to be alone. You've always been exceptional at your job, and I've admired you for it. Between the two of us, you've always been the smarter one." Fernando took a deep breath. "Just find him alive. I know you can do it, my dear brother."

- "I will, Fer. Trust me, I will." Just then, Manuel's phone rang. He attempted to silence it.

- "Answer it; it might be important," Fernando said as he walked away.

Meanwhile, reporters covering the scene snapped photos and took wide-angle shots of the chaos that had engulfed the area. Some news outlets interrupted regular programming to broadcast live updates. As the city's Governor arrived, his close relationship with the Senator became the focus. Reporters crowded around him, vying for statements.

With practiced composure, Manuel announced he would make one general statement.

- "The C4 security cameras in Mexico City have provided us with critical data. We've identified the vehicle the suspected kidnappers used to flee eastward."

- "Wasn't it the same one found burning a few blocks from here, Governor?" a voice from the crowd asked.

- "Yes, it was," Manuel confirmed. "However, we've already collected DNA samples, hair, and partial fingerprints from the scorched vehicle," he said, pausing briefly—knowing full well it was a fabrication, but necessary for the narrative. "I can assure you we're close to locating Senator Raúl Pérez."

- "Governor," another reporter, a heavyset man, interjected, "there are rumors this is tied to a political dirty war over the General Telecommunications Law reform. Any comments?"

- "There are many theories, but it's too soon to speculate. Whoever is responsible will face the full weight of the law."

- "Have you been in contact with the President, the Attorney General's Office, or the National Security Commission?"

- "All government bodies at every level are working tirelessly and in coordination. I've communicated with everyone involved in the investigation. As President Trevilla said, this is an attack on the Mexican State and the rule of law. We will continue working to clarify this incident, just as we do with every crime. I ask for your patience. At 6 PM, I'll hold a press conference to provide further updates."

Manuel then walked back toward Senator Pérez Irigoyen, placing a hand on his shoulder and whispering something inaudible to the press and onlookers. Photographers seized the moment, capturing what many believed would be the next day's headline image.

Traffic officers reopened the thoroughfare. The Governor headed toward the National Nutrition Institute, his entourage dispersing as transit officers escorted the Senator's family to their vehicle.

Back in his office, Alejandro Harlington finally arrived. His secretary immediately handed him a message written on a card. Reading it quietly, he observed the bustling activity around him. Staff worked relentlessly to piece together any profiles or images, scrutinizing every detail. The ballistics lab analyzed striation patterns from firearm barrels but found no matches with criminal records from the past five years. Doubt and urgency loomed as Harlington reread the message, trying to decipher its implications.

Meanwhile, the Senator, his mother, and his sister declined a police escort and opted to use Fernando's Mercedes-Benz instead. Accompanied by a security convoy, they headed west, then north, toward Las Arboledas. As they passed through Polanco, an uneasy silence filled the car. Fernando's thoughts drifted until something caught his attention—a yellow "caution" tape blocking access to a pedestrian bridge staircase about twenty meters from where his father's vehicle had been found that morning.

8. Safe House, Sierra de Santa Catarina, Mexico City; 2:42 PM, July 30th.

Lost in thought, I stood motionless, trapped in the interminable wait. *El Tinaco* offered me a drink. I accepted it, letting the liquid cool my throat. Then he invited me to play a hand of poker. I smiled faintly and declined, saying I wasn't in the mood. I preferred to rest for a while. My gaze drifted to the horizon as memories surfaced. The weight of a single bullet still lingered in my mind. A wave of anxiety washed over me as I glanced at the old man I'd kidnapped just hours earlier. My thoughts wandered back in time, and a faint smile crept across my face.

It was true—after the murder of *El Gato*, I had to flee north. In time, I earned the respect of many hitmen and bosses, both in Mexico and during occasional incursions into the United States. They still called me *El Pasa* over there. I must have spent two or three years in that world. The routine blurs details; days meld into weeks, weeks into months, and years lose all meaning. I can only describe my time there as a whirlwind adventure, always in the line of fire, always active in "the business."

I'm certain it was shortly after the 1994 crisis. That's one detail that stands out—the devaluation hit me while I was in Monterrey. The "Tequila Effect" taught everyone, even us outlaws, to tighten our belts. I must admit I was never entirely sure if it was the "December mistake" or something else. Whether Salinas or Zedillo was to blame didn't really matter. What mattered was how the crisis struck the country like a bucket of ice water. One day, I found myself holding a ten *nuevos pesos* bill—blue with Pancho Villa's face and a yellow corn cob.

I must have been 15 or 16. Those were my drifter years. I traveled all over northern Mexico. Nostalgia tugs at me when I recall running through Monterrey's Cuauhtémoc Avenue, darting from one pawn shop to another to exchange gold chains, a few dollars, or some low-value watches. My memories of that chaotic yet oddly sentimental time remain vivid. Back then, I always seemed to be running—thin, with sunken eyes, and never gaining a pound, no matter what I did.

During that phase of my life, I dove headfirst into gambling. It was risky since it was illegal, like almost everything else I'd done up to that point. Gambling did bring me some money—though not as much as I wanted. And the cost was always high: betting your life, along with everything else. Gambling inevitably creates enemies, especially with those who win less than you. By my second year in Monterrey, I had more enemies than I could count. Police protection grew more difficult—and expensive—particularly since I'd already clashed with the two most powerful commanders in the city. Every conflict in the city seemed to land squarely on my shoulders. My presence had become inconvenient for everyone.

After a bar fight—one of many—one of the commanders caught me red-handed with stolen cash, drugs, and a few trinkets. When he shoved me into the patrol car, he reminded me of his earlier warnings. He told me plainly: if I stayed involved in anything else, he'd make sure I disappeared. The message was clear: leave, or they'd ship me off somewhere I wouldn't return from.

I wasn't scared, but the three neurons rattling around in my brain back then told me "the other side" wasn't an option. So I decided to respect their territory. Every place has its allies and its enemies.

During my time in Monterrey, I met people who became a kind of family. One of them was Guillermo Marín, who everyone called *El Tío* (The Uncle). Guillermo was a retired general who worked with various cartels, shuttling between the Golden Triangle and Monterrey. He was older, sharp, and pragmatic—a man who always had a word of encouragement, even for those outside his inner circle. I was introduced to him by a cocaine distributor near Fundidora Park. From the start, we hit it off, perhaps because we were both from Mexico City.

In a world where being a *chilango* was a liability, finding someone from the same place felt like a small victory.

Guillermo eventually proposed I go with him to Tijuana, which he affectionately called "the biggest brothel in the world." He claimed to have a series of businesses where I could be useful. He taught me to handle firearms with precision, financed a pair of pistols for me, and hooked me up with ammo at good prices. He assured me that as long as I wanted to work for him, I'd always have a job. At first, I thought he was joking. Over time, I realized he wasn't.

Guillermo was no older than 45 back then—a benevolent but reckless man. After leaving the military, he became more approachable. Though the military often works hand in glove with organized crime, working directly for them wasn't well-regarded—people often accused their associates of being snitches or traitors.

A friend once told me Guillermo was both feared and powerful. He controlled not only the local and state police—who were especially terrified of him—but also had influence with federal agents, military personnel, and even the Navy. My friend Agustín, who worked as a petty thief, claimed Guillermo had saved him from prison numerous times. Agustín had warned me early on that I'd need a "godfather" to survive in Monterrey. I didn't understand the concept at first. But when Guillermo saved my life during a random street encounter, I realized how crucial he was.

One day, a rival tried to run me down with a red Ford Cougar. Furious over losing his share of the "business," he came after me. If it hadn't been for Guillermo's intervention, I'd have been dead under the car's wheels. That incident cemented our bond. He adopted me, teaching me discipline and the art of survival. Under his mentorship, I learned to kill from a distance and earned respect as one of his most reliable men.

Hours after Commander Piña's threats, I visited Guillermo at his house in Garza García. It was an immaculate space, though his reputation for stinginess was evident in the cheap liquor he served. After some back-and-forth, I told him of my decision to go to Tijuana.

He studied me intently, then asked a chilling question:

"How many have you taken down, kid?"

Something deep inside me felt ashamed because I didn't know exactly how many I had killed. I looked at him with some unease, shrugged, and sighed. Then, I just looked into his eyes, shrugged again to signal my ignorance, and stood still for a moment, waiting for him to scold me or tell me that what I had done was the most immoral thing he had ever seen or heard of. Instead, he burst into a loud laugh.

"That always happens, kid," he said, chuckling. "Sooner or later, you lose count."

I laughed too, unsure why I was doing it.

Marín smiled like someone who had found something long sought after. He patted me on the shoulder and handed me some money, instructing me to head to the *Fundidora* the next day to find "Agustín." Agustín would provide information, bus fare, and directions to a decent-enough motel on the outskirts of García. Then, Marín added, "I knew the moment I saw you, you'd end up in my Tijuana business."

"Come on, you deserve better. You're a dumb kid, sure, but that's something we can fix," he said, downing his aguardiente, which he was drinking out of a mug. "You can tell who's not as dumb by their eyes. People like you, who've killed, can't look straight anymore. That gives them away."

He pulled out some cash and a business card from his wallet and told me to travel by land to Tijuana. Upon arrival, I was to go to a place called "Jake Mate," a dive frequented by American sex tourists—a fact I'd only learn later. There, I was to ask for Wally, who would know what to do with me.

The next morning, I left for Tijuana and never returned to Monterrey.

I barely recall the journey, except for fleeting images: stops along the way, glimpses of the desert landscape of northern Mexico. I didn't speak to anyone during the long hours of bus rides. While some people might struggle with such solitude, I learned to enjoy it. As the miles flew by, I wondered what exactly I'd be doing when I reached the final Spanish-speaking outpost of the continent.

I saw things I'd never imagined and entered a world of unexpected circumstances on that trip, which was far from being touristy. Ciudad Juárez left an impression on me with its endless sand dunes, a city that never seemed to sleep, and its constant flow of people. At the time, the boom of factories was in full swing, with maquiladoras producing shoes, clothing, and high-tech components like printer cables and refrigerators. Many factories were still under construction. Back then, the infamous "Juárez women" hadn't become public knowledge. Although I was there for only a few hours, the place struck me as a constellation of stars.

When I arrived in Tijuana, I headed straight to "Jake Mate." Finding the elusive Wally proved almost impossible since I arrived at noon—a time when the bar's administrator was nowhere to be found. His nickname, Wally, came from everyone asking, "Where's Wally?"—a nod to the popular *Where's Waldo?* books. Back in Monterrey, I'd spent hours with those red, blue, or yellow-covered books, scanning every page for the striped-hat figure. The moment one of Wally's subordinates mentioned the nickname, I knew exactly who they were referring to.

With no other options, I wandered through Tijuana's colorful but hostile streets. Its graffiti-covered walls and clusters of Latin American migrants wandering around the center gave it a unique, contrasting atmosphere. I didn't yet understand what "cultural contrasts" meant, but that's precisely what I was experiencing. Elderly American tourists with limited, heavily-accented Spanish roamed the streets freely, seeking legal drugs or spending their dollars on random trinkets.

Around them, men and women from every corner of Mexico loitered, waiting for any chance to cross the border and chase the American dream.

Tijuana is a quintessential *Sin City*, colorful and embodying the authentic identity of Latin America's last frontier. Even for someone familiar with Mexico City's immensity, Tijuana feels amplified in every way. This border divides every conceivable ideology, giving the city its unique character—a mix of allure and repulsion. I didn't fully grasp this on my first encounter, though. Instead, I used my money to grab some food and drink while soaking in the unusual urban landscape. The best thing about Tijuana? No one saw me as just another outsider—because, in truth, everyone there was.

As the sun set, I retraced my steps to the neon-lit corner where "Jake Mate" stood. Green and blue lights from the sign bathed the pavement, guiding customers to the bar. At the door, a bouncer asked me something I didn't quite catch. I showed him the card Marín had given me and mumbled that I needed to see Wally. He motioned for me to follow him through the bar, leading to a shadowy staircase.

I climbed the metal stairs, the kind used to access rooftops, and arrived at a heavy iron door. Another man stopped me there. As I waited, I peered through a strategically placed window, observing the bar's activity from above. After a brief exchange, the bouncer allowed us inside a small office furnished with two worn-out chairs, a heavy steel desk from the 1940s, and a single dim bulb.

Behind the desk sat a man who welcomed me, extended his hand, and dismissed the others. Once we were alone, he said:

- "So, you're the little chilango hitman, huh?"

- "Yes," I replied with as much confidence as I could muster. "Marín sent me to assist you wherever you need."

- "To *assist* me, huh?" he repeated mockingly. "Well, I don't need much help, but since the *Tío* sent you, I suppose I'll take you in. He probably told you he runs things around here."

"He told me what I needed to know," I lied. "I'm at your service, as he instructed. If you don't want to give me orders, I'll call him for guidance."

He crossed his arms, waited for me to finish my pitch, and then said coldly: "Never say the boss's name. Never."

Lighting a cigar, he added, "I know your whole story, kid. You're nothing special, just another wannabe killer. But since Marín sent you, let's see what you've got. Tomorrow, Guti will take you to the shooting range. Twelve rounds of twenty-five. I imagine you've been trained, but I need to see it myself before I assign you any real tasks."

He handed me a Glock 17 with a silencer—a weapon I'd never seen before—and warned me not to use it for anything outside the business. "If you mess up, you'll ruin it," he said.

That night, I lay awake, thinking about the gun, the training ahead, and the new life awaiting me. Something told me my world was about to change irreversibly.

Calderón de la Barca y Masaryk, Polanco. Mexico City. 4:30 p.m., July 30th.

Alicia Bahena was a woman not easily perturbed. This had been her nature for years—perhaps since her youth. Her childhood had been filled with suffering, most notably the trauma of being violated by her father's brother. That experience had scarred her deeply, making her unlike the other women in her family. Alicia was strong, resolute, and unyielding. Once, when asked what she feared, she had replied, "*Nothing at all. The worst has already happened.*" Cold and calculating, she could be intelligent and ruthless when the situation called for it. Yet, deep inside, she knew there was one thing she feared above all else: losing the man who was the source of her life and luxury.

Raúl Pérez had been her lover for over a decade. He had always been a handsome man, though age had taken its toll. Still, he was more than just good looks; he marketed himself as a cultured, well-educated gentleman. Owner of a prominent electrical generation company and a high-ranking government official during two administrations, he was, by all accounts, the perfect man. Married, yes—but who could complain? As his partner, Alicia enjoyed all the advantages: a man who had never lied to her and whose worst flaw was his unapologetic cynicism, which, in truth, complemented her own nature.

Alicia paced the spacious living room of her Polanco apartment, restless and unable to find solace. Her mind raced with terrible ideas, images, and memories. The apartment—something she could never have obtained without Raúl—was a testament to his generosity. Three years ago, he had surprised her by purchasing it as a birthday gift. That night, he had organized the most romantic dinner she could recall. Raúl had always convinced her, in his way, that he truly loved her. Their getaways to Toronto, trips to Paris, unforgettable beach vacations, and countless shared anecdotes made him the man of her life.

Alicia had been married once, though she could barely remember the man or the relationship—a complete mistake in her life choices. Raúl wasn't even the first married man she had dated. As a teenager, she had sought out older men, hoping they would provide for her and her younger siblings. Her list of conquests included dozens of older men, though most were cheap barflies, stingy, and foul-smelling. Perhaps it was that string of poor choices that drove her to marry a seemingly decent man, only to find disappointment. Her search for stability eventually led her to a job working for Raúl Pérez.

As his secretary, Alicia had insight into every aspect of Raúl's daily life. She knew the sources of his income and how he managed them. Over time, their professional relationship evolved into a romantic one. Raúl trusted her implicitly, even allowing her to manage the finances of Fernando, his eldest son and pride and joy. Few people earned such trust, but it came with a price. Alicia received significant financial benefits for overseeing his family's finances, enabling her to pay for her mother's cancer treatment and secure a house in Cotija, Michoacán—a property she was still paying off and would be for another 20 years.

Earlier that day, Alicia had watched the news of the attack on Raúl on television. At first, it felt surreal, like something detached from her reality. She even considered the possibility that it was a staged event to bolster Fernando's presidential campaign. But as she thought about it, she realized Raúl would have confided in her if that were the case, sharing every detail, no matter how insignificant.

As she paced like a caged lion in her apartment, clutching her phone, she debated calling Fernando under the pretext of offering information as Raúl's secretary. But she hesitated. Valeria, Raúl's daughter, would be there—a woman who had always viewed Alicia as nothing more than *the other woman*. Alicia wasn't in the mood to endure the family's disdain or humiliation. Besides, she knew they suspected her, particularly when Raúl was unusually eager to travel for "business."

Dressed in a black tailored suit—chosen as if she were heading to an executive meeting—Alicia felt the weight of her fears pressing down on her. The possibility that Raúl, the man who had sustained her lifestyle and her mother's treatment, might be truly gone—or worse, dead—was unbearable. She tried to push the thought away, distracting herself with anything else, but it was futile.

Her anxiety only deepened as she checked their shared bank accounts, finding no unusual activity. This only reinforced her fear that the attack was no mere publicity stunt.

The news channel continued its relentless coverage, filling her mind with images of helicopters, the President's address, and the chaos surrounding the black Lincoln on Periférico Sur. She couldn't help but wonder about Raúl's fate. Would he be tortured? Killed? And what would become of her? The thought of being "old," abandoned, and destitute haunted her.

Alicia ran her fingers over the lines and wrinkles on her face as she stood before the living room mirror. She wasn't the teenager who could charm her way into anything with a simple smile. Pulling at her temples, she momentarily saw a glimpse of her younger self, but the sagging skin of her neck quickly reminded her of the truth.

Earlier, she had called some of Raúl's friends—men they had dined with or traveled with on business trips. Two hadn't even answered. Another had dismissed her concerns, claiming he knew no more than she did. With dwindling hope, she reached out to Julián Alaminos, a close family friend and one of the fiercest opponents of her relationship with Raúl. Alaminos, a shrewd lawyer and Raúl's son's godfather, had always been cold toward her. Though Alicia suspected he harbored some secret desire for her, his disdain was palpable.

Now, standing alone in her apartment, Alicia was consumed by a mix of fear and self-preservation. Her thoughts weren't solely about

Raúl's safety but also about her own future—about the wealth, power, and security he had provided. In the shadow of uncertainty, Alicia realized the precariousness of her position, teetering between love, dependency, and survival.

She knew it, too, from the way he looked at her—always a sly glance at her neckline, a wandering gaze down her legs, and, when he thought no one was watching, a furtive, vulgar, and obscene stare at her back. Yet, despite all this, the lawyer was an old sea dog, a seasoned player who would never admit to such things. Alicia kept this knowledge to herself, as most women do about things men will never confess to liking. She considered using this unspoken understanding to her advantage, thinking it might give her a real opportunity—perhaps not just a bargaining chip but something akin to a blank check.

She had kept Alaminos' phone number since their last of only three encounters in nearly seven years of acquaintance. It was, in fact, his business card she had saved. Alicia vividly recalled the tension she felt when accepting it from the esteemed lawyer, both of them assuming they would never actually use it. That assumption might have held true had it not been for the dire and desperate nature of this particular case.

Alicia picked up her home phone, copied down the number, and hoped it hadn't changed over time. As she dialed, her heart raced, unsure if it was because she was calling a man she knew harbored feelings for her or because of the weight of the issue she was about to discuss. After a few rings, a deep, masculine voice answered with a hint of surprise.

There was a moment of hesitation before she responded, but Alicia finally gathered herself. In a firm, steady voice, she said:

"Licenciado Alaminos, you may not recognize my name—I'm an acquaintance of yours." She paused cautiously before continuing, "I've been in a relationship with Raúl Pérez for many years. We met at a restaurant some time ago. My name is Alicia..."

"Forgive me, my memory isn't very good," the voice replied firmly. "But tell me, how can I assist you?"

The lawyer was lying—she could tell instantly. He didn't fool her for a moment with his claim of forgetfulness. Lawyers, after all, are masters of pretense and selective amnesia when it suits them, though rarely skilled enough to deceive a woman.

After several minutes of futile conversation, during which the lawyer seemed to hope she would give up on establishing their prior connection, he finally admitted to knowing who she was. Even so, his tone remained "polite" as he asked again how he could help her.

Alicia hesitated. A part of her knew exactly what she wanted from the deep-voiced lawyer. She took a deep breath and made a bold request:

"I want to know if you can keep me informed about the situation with my—" She faltered briefly, unsure of what to call Raúl: husband, boyfriend, or simply a friend? The hesitation led to an awkward pause, followed by a moment of profound silence.

Alaminos inhaled deeply before finally speaking, his words sharp and deliberate:

"How could you think me capable of such immorality?" he rebuked forcefully. "Let me make myself clear... Madam, I have been a friend of Raúl's family for over forty years. What you're asking would be a fatal betrayal, an unforgivable breach of trust. I cannot, in good conscience, undermine the trust of Mariela or her children. You must also know that I cannot judge Raúl's actions—he is like a brother to me. But I do not condone his behavior toward his family."

Alicia felt a strong urge to hang up and leave the lawyer speaking to an empty line, but she restrained herself. She had learned that to achieve anything, someone like her had to be tolerant, patient, and even indulgent toward the comments and offenses of others. In a gentle tone, she said:

"The first to know how wrong this is, is me. I also want you to know that I take full responsibility for this mess—I know it's my fault. But no one can judge love, for it's love that has placed us in this situation. And precisely because of this immeasurable love, I ask you to do this for us—for Raúl and me."

Alicia paused, and the silence on the line grew heavy. Finally, she let slip the words she knew might sway the man on the other end of the call:

"I will find a way to repay you, whatever the cost," she said, her tone shifting slightly. "Anything you ask of me in return for this favor."

Julián Alaminos pretended not to hear the last part of her plea and offered a response crafted with the finesse of a man experienced in life but more cunning than courteous.

"My apologies," he said in a measured, almost neutral tone. "The number appearing on my caller ID—is that your mobile number?" Alicia replied that it wasn't; it was her home phone. She then shared her mobile number with him, which he duly noted. Alaminos promised to call her back in forty-five minutes with any information he could gather.

Golf Club La Hacienda, State of Mexico. 4:40 PM, July 30th.

The hollow, gray voice that had contacted Mariela to inform her that her husband had been kidnapped had yet to call back or make any demands for his return. Time dragged on interminably, yet the clock kept ticking. For Raúl's wife, who hadn't moved from her son Fernando's shoulder, hope was fading. She couldn't help but imagine finding Raúl's mutilated body abandoned in some remote, unfamiliar place—far from the home that had once welcomed him back with open arms. They had shared so many moments together as a family.

Now, as she observed that Fernando had grown taller and stronger than his father, a sense of pride filled her heart. Her son, now the man of the house, patiently cradled her head against his shoulder, sharing her sighs. Despite his position as a Senator, Fernando had set aside the polished veneer of his office to be there for his mother, bridging the emotional distance that politics had imposed between him, his sister, and their family.

Both mother and son were lost in memories of the past. Fernando reminisced about childhood days spent with his sister and their dogs, while Mariela's thoughts traveled further back to when her youth hadn't yet been stolen by the cruel passage of time. Life hadn't been perfect, but it had been good—idyllic, even, in many ways. Mariela had always been committed to maintaining the image of a perfect family, a role instilled in her by her upbringing and one she had faithfully upheld.

But holding on to composure was no easy feat when everything seemed to be falling apart. Adding to the chaos was the circus-like presence of federal agents swarming through their home. To Mariela, it felt as if hundreds of strangers were continuously moving between the living room and the dining area, reducing their privacy to a bare minimum. Computer screens displayed incomprehensible coordinates and triangulated maps. Equipment was being assembled, mounted into metal cabinets, and arranged in place of her dining table and china cabinet. Yet, despite the frenzy, progress was nonexistent.

The private line on the Senator's phone rang. Fernando glanced at the screen, recognizing the name of his father's lawyer and his own godfather, Julián Alaminos. Earlier, Fernando had thought of calling him, as he often did in difficult times. However, this time, the coincidence felt almost telepathic. Julián, always calm and capable, seemed to possess a preternatural understanding of crises. Fernando had refrained from reaching out, determined not to burden him unnecessarily. But now, hearing the familiar voice of his godfather filled him with a sense of relief.

Julián's grave voice provided advice and offered to join the family during this trying time. Fernando, feeling a secret comfort, warmly reassured him, "You know, godfather, you're always welcome here—especially now." His words soothed both Mariela and his sister, who trusted that Julián's presence would bring much-needed support.

From her seat on the loveseat, Mariela overheard the conversation as she sipped her tea. The rain had finally stopped, leaving the air crisp and the sounds around her sharper. Her mind wandered uncontrollably, replaying scenes from the past. She could see, as vividly as if it were happening before her eyes, afternoons when her children were young and gathered around the dining table to do their homework. She recalled the chaos of friends coming over, the thrill of first loves, and, most vividly, the day of Fernando's wedding—a day he preferred not to remember.

Back then, *we were so happy*, she thought. A sudden realization struck her: *When did we resign ourselves to this solitude and suffering?* The thought deepened the furrow in her brow, an unspoken question she couldn't share with those around her.

Fernando's marriage to Lucía, his high school sweetheart, had lasted only two fleeting years. The rumor was that she had caught him with another woman in his office, a claim Fernando never clarified to anyone—least of all his mother. To Mariela, Lucía had been the ideal wife: distinguished, beautiful, intelligent, and devout in her faith. When the couple had wed, they had made so many plans—children, a house, travels—but politics had derailed everything. Fernando's relentless ambition to become President consumed him, a shared dream with his father that drew them closer but pushed everyone else away.

For Mariela, the breakup was heartbreaking. Lucía had been a symbol of stability, and her absence left a void. Yet, Fernando still thought of her often. Like many men, half in love and half obsessed, he believed she was still within reach, though he didn't know how or when he might win her back. Publicly, he appeared in magazines alongside models or actresses—part of a calculated effort advised by his political strategist to build his public image. Mariela, however, saw through the charade, understanding it was merely a ploy for publicity.

Meanwhile, Raúl openly celebrated Fernando's media presence, proudly showing off articles featuring his son, despite the superficial nature of such fame.

Valeria, Fernando's sister, faced her own struggles in her dysfunctional marriage. Her husband, a textile entrepreneur, spent half the year abroad, claiming it was necessary for the business—a pretext she reluctantly accepted. Mariela had instilled in Valeria the same ideals of being a perfect, submissive wife, a role she dutifully fulfilled despite her husband's prolonged absences. Fernando, however, resented his brother-in-law and the liberties he took. Deep down, he was pained by his sister's silent suffering but felt powerless to intervene.

As Fernando sat beside his mother amidst the chaos of agents and equipment, his thoughts once again turned to Lucía. The memories burned brightly in his mind, leaving him disoriented. He knew he had to focus on the present, but controlling his thoughts was a battle in itself. Glancing at his mother, he wondered what was running through her mind as she sat surrounded by the storm of activity. The answer, perhaps, was buried in her silence, as her memories painted a bittersweet portrait of a life that once seemed perfect.

- "Fer, do you remember when we were kids and used to play hide-and-seek?" Valeria asked, a nostalgic smile lighting up her face as she finished the sentence.

- "Of course," the Senator replied, gesturing toward a specific spot. "I always hid in the pantry... though I never understood how you kept finding me."

- "That's true. You were such a fool," Valeria teased, grinning. "But you never figured out where I hid, did you?"

- "No, never," Fernando admitted, meeting her gaze. "I honestly thought you'd just vanished."

- "I was in Mom's closet," Valeria said conspiratorially, "behind that little gadget we used to keep the air dry."

- "Oh, my God, I never would've guessed that," Fernando breathed deeply, taking it in. "Do you remember that time I almost fell off the roof while we were playing with Daniela, my cousin? It was almost dark by then."

- "I never knew about that!" Mariela exclaimed indignantly.

- "Mom," Valeria chimed in with mock exasperation, "obviously, we weren't going to tell you that Fer almost got himself killed. Those kinds of things don't exactly come up during dinner."

- "I remember, though," Valeria said, laughing. "You were such a little runt back then."

- "Compared to you, I've always been a runt," Fernando quipped with equal sarcasm. "Hey, have you heard anything about your friend Selene lately?"

- "No... no idea," Valeria replied, her tone deepening. "It's been ages since I've talked to any of my friends. Married life takes over everything. Why do you ask?"

- "No reason," Fernando said, brushing off the question. "She just popped into my mind. She was always beautiful, wasn't she?"

- "Oh, Fernando," Valeria groaned. "Look at everything going on, and that's what's on your mind?"

- "Alright, sorry," the Senator murmured sheepishly. "I just wanted to change the subject. You all know I hate waiting."

The conversation drifted into lighthearted banter, an attempt to dissipate the tension caused by the slow passage of time and the absence of any news about the man who had been kidnapped.

11. 2nd Closed Street, Camino a las Minas, Sierra de Santa Catarina, Iztapalapa, Mexico City. 5:00 PM, July 30th.

We had eaten, as we always did, like a family—because that's the way things are done in the "business." Tinaco, Chucho, two other men whose names I never knew, and a woman, who I understood would be the one feeding the kidnapped man. The same man who was now sitting just a few feet from me, his hands bound, his mouth stuffed with cotton cloth, his eyes blindfolded, his legs tied. He didn't move, but I could hear his heavy breathing. As I watched him from a distance, trying not to make a sound, I thought about getting closer and asking him something, but that would be against the rules.

For a brief moment, I imagined that everyone present would agree that we should leave the house. Tinaco and I had things to do. The first was to collect payment from the contact who had hired the service, the other was to plan a new life. As far as my part went, I intended to leave again, to head down an unknown path. Tinaco, I wasn't sure about. I didn't care what he wanted to do. But right in the middle of our meal, we were told that things were complicated, and that we should stay, at least for a while longer. The boss had ordered it, and as it was logical, half the world was looking for us at that very moment. I wasn't worried. We had taken some precautions. Two days before the attack, a little over fifty hours ago, we had vandalized the cameras that could have captured our actions. We'd covered our faces, brought weapons with us, and anything that could contain traces or DNA.

Two of the men explained, as they came and went, looking for any kind of tracking operation, that we would be fine with them. I assessed the situation and thought that, for the first time in a long while, I considered it a wise idea. I glanced at Tinaco, whose expression remained as blank as ever. He nodded slightly. Someone in front of us asked why they called him "Tinaco." I found that question absurd. No one asks such a thing in this world—why someone is called this or that. To me, it was obvious that the name came from the fact that he was big and fat, like a large black plastic rotomolded water tank. But I said nothing, merely listening to what I assumed would be a brief explanation from Tinaco.

"I was born in the water tanks," he said, pointing in a specific direction. "Here, in Santa Catarina. I remember when the fields were still green and fertile, before all these damn houses piled up on top of each other, full of decay and infested with useless people. Yes, those. The ones who now live in these barren hills, filled with gray, cramped buildings. Those fields, they were once lush and beautiful spaces. When it rained, they would turn green again, and it looked like a different place, like a better prairie."

Then, everything became more complicated. There was a time when nothing was like it is now. Those who came to invade the hills would machete anyone who crossed what they claimed were their lands, which they divided with stones, crates, and scraps of wood and plastic. You would see the kids in their underwear, dividing up their little patches of land, and the women, they were brave. They would bring out the brazier, and if they didn't have a machete to defend themselves, they would burn you with the hot coals.

The man, who had been passionately telling the story of the land that had witnessed his birth, stopped and thought for a moment, as though recalling something that wasn't entirely clear. Finally, he said, "And watch out, you might trip over one of the stones that marked the boundaries of the shacks; you could really hurt yourself. As for me, since I was a kid, I've been a big guy, and once, three of them chased me down and gave me a beating. And later, when I grew up, I turned out like a big water tank, huge, fat, and dark." The group smiled at the confession of how he got his nickname.

I smiled too when he finished his story, and I looked at the man with the yellowish hands and permanent dark circles under his eyes. There was something in his face that resembled a smile, coming from his thick, slightly purplish lips and the crooked, yellowish teeth that completed it. I stared at him, rediscovering him, noticing his rebellious hair—messy from birth, standing up and tangled—his deep, dark eyes, and his sparse eyebrows, shaped in a slightly comical way. Then, with patience, he turned to a young man named Chucho and began speaking to him, telling his story.

"I started in this 'business' out of necessity," he paused, scratched his head, and confessed, "I would have liked to study and be someone different, but I'm not ashamed of who I am... In the end, we are what we can afford to be. My mom always said I needed to make sure my little brothers had their milk, something to eat, a taco, and in search of that taco, being the oldest, I found a way to help. You know, by stealing a grill, a mirror... then, when the 'coflas' took over this region, they invited me in and gave me my weapon. That's how it went for a long time. Later, I had to leave for Tijuana, where I met the crazy guys and other transnational mafias, though those damn gringos say the bad guys are just from the south side of the border. But the truth is, it's not like that; the Maras and the people born on that side come and beat us up badly." He paused, looking at me, pointing at me, to which I just smiled back honestly.

"And you, Pasa? How did you get into all of this?" Chucho asked, looking into my eyes with a mixture of doubt and excitement. I returned the gaze to the young man who had been eating with us, his eyes full of curiosity. I looked at him with a bit of strangeness, as if wondering about something inexplicable. I glanced at the others at the table and decided to tell them that I didn't remember how it had all started. It couldn't have been much different from my friend Tinaco's story—we were from the same generation, things were different back then, there were other standards, and we identified more with each other.

The truth was that it happened in a life that was very different from the one I was living lately. I added that it had been so many years ago that I could hardly recall it. Chucho looked at me disappointed, but didn't ask further, probably because he feared getting scolded by Tinaco or because he thought I simply didn't want to tell my story. I got up from the table and thanked them for the meal. The woman came over and told me that if I needed anything, I should just let her know. I moved just a few steps and sat down on a chair, which was surprisingly comfortable considering how bad the conditions seemed.

I lied to them; I remembered every single event as though it had happened the day before. Life hadn't been easy in Tijuana. During the first few weeks, my days began at four in the morning. For some reason I never quite understood, I'd go out running through the dark streets of that city of colorful murals, graffiti on every corner, and nearly empty streets. I always ran with my head hidden under a cap or the hoodie of my sweatshirt—seven and a half kilometers, that's what Guti and Wally had recommended. Sometimes, I ran alongside other men who worked for Wally. After finishing the run, we'd go for breakfast, always an oatmeal smoothie, and after that, we'd be given physical tasks.

We generally had to load chairs and tables into the bar, as well as any merchandise that arrived, which we unloaded into the warehouse next to the "Jake Mate." Sometimes, there was also other merchandise to be "served" at the establishment, and we had to repack or bottle it. In the afternoons, we were responsible for securing the surrounding streets, and at night, we'd throw out drunk customers and keep the peace at the "Jake Mate." There were days when you could hardly sleep, yet for some reason, I remember enjoying it. I liked my new position. In this city, there were fewer issues with the police, the control of the place practically belonged to us, and that was very good because all it took was for no one to step out of line, as Wally used to say.

That was my life during the first few months of my adventure in Tijuana. It was after the first six months of this routine that Wally, in person, assigned me my first important job—an incursion, he said. "You need to be careful. And this is because, in the end, you turned out to be not just a loudmouthed braggart, but you've got some brains too. I'll give credit to the old man, he knows how to pick the right people to work with."

The task was to find an American named Robert Q. James. I later learned that the "Q" stood for Quintell, and according to Wally, this man owed a lot of money to the house, and that was unacceptable. "If someone finds out we let these losers owe us money like this fool, everyone will want to do the same. This is a matter of respect, so you need to bring him to me." My job was to bring him before him and develop a method to make him understand he needed to pay the debt, plus a small commission for Wally and me. Wally gave me a few photographs of the man I needed to bring to the "Jake Mate" and the keys to a van used for transporting goods to the bar. By then, I knew it was a brothel and a drug den that exploited minors, with its primary clientele being crazy Americans who thought this lawless land with no future was made for their enjoyment and pleasure.

I drove the van that same morning and went out with my weapon to get the crazy gringo to pay. I had permission to use any method to make sure he paid. I spent hours driving around the streets where I was told I might find him. By noon, I was getting a bit tired of searching for the old debtor, but since it was my first important job, I knew I couldn't give up. Fortunately, I found him at a pharmacy buying painkillers and opiates. It wasn't uncommon—back then, many old Americans came to Mexico to fill their prescriptions because it was much cheaper than doing it in California. And those who didn't have prescriptions always had a good friend named Benjamin Franklin to help them.

I followed him quietly to a Ford Ranger from 1982, sand-colored, a bit dirty with a minor scratch, and with worn-out black upholstery.

When he opened the driver's door, I pointed my gun at him and told him to give me the keys and get in without saying a word. I ordered him to move over to the passenger seat, slowly. He obeyed, keeping his hands raised near his head. I told him not to play dumb and lower his hands, knowing he was keeping them there in case a cop came by and saw him with a gun pointed at him.

I got in and started the engine. The man, with his white hair, glasses, and ridiculous flower-patterned white shirt with a red background, asked me what I was going to do with him. I replied that I was just transporting him to the "Jake Mate" so he could pay his debt. My job was to schedule appointments, and I couldn't give him more information. He sat down and took a deep breath, telling me he didn't have the money but that he was working on a big deal and would soon pay all his debts. He never turned his head toward me, always speaking while looking straight ahead. His attitude annoyed me, and I found it rude.

The trip lasted no more than ten minutes. At the loading door, in front of the maneuvering yard where we brought the merchandise into the bar, I stopped the truck and honked. Three men quickly opened the door and allowed the vehicle inside. Once inside, with three other workers from "Jake Mate," we tied him to a chair. It was then that I learned how to tie strong knots to withstand the strength of a 1.80-meter tall man. As soon as we finished, Wally came down from his office to the spot where we had the debtor. He told us to leave; his job was done, he said. "This one's on me," he added. I never heard from that American again. The truck stayed there for a few months, then was repainted black. When that happened, Wally told me, "You can use it. It's partly your payment for bringing in Quintell. That old bastard was despicable. I reported to your godfather, my 'Partner,' how well you're doing."

My first job had ended successfully, and from then on, I focused on locating debtors for Wally. I never knew what happened to any of them, whether they came back to the streets, alive or dead. But at least four dozen similar jobs were assigned to me in the four years I lived in Tijuana. The pay was good and directly depended on the amount owed by the individuals I tracked down, usually on the Mexican side of town, though sometimes I crossed the border, capturing some unlucky soul in Calexico or San Diego. The risk was higher there, though, because the police were incorruptible—at least that's what I thought at first.

I collected from drug dealers, robbers, even kidnapped Americans—both men and women. Mostly men, usually older, who crossed to have a bit of fun with the prostitutes Wally managed, who were largely the responsibility of Guti. The kidnappings varied, depending on the situation and the victim's ability to pay. Some lasted only a few hours, while others, like a man named Johnson, lasted seven weeks in the Jake Mate warehouse. I recovered all kinds of merchandise—living and dead, from drugs and weapons to women. And God, I wish I had never encountered her, because she was the woman who became my undoing.

Yamila was a sixteen-year-old with blue eyes, though she looked at least twenty. Back then, I couldn't pinpoint her accent and continually mistook her for a southern girl—so that's what we called her. She wasn't the only one at "Jake Mate." There were many women from Central and South America offering their services. Yamila fascinated me from the moment I saw her—her jet-black hair, as intense as her beautifully proportioned body. She wasn't very tall, which made her even more beautiful. I had seen her at the bar before, but it wasn't until one afternoon when I found her in the filthy apartments on the roof that I attempted to speak to her. I knew her room was just three away from mine. I had never spoken to her before, and when I tried, I froze completely. It was so ridiculous that she laughed and walked away before I could even greet her. Never once did it cross my mind that she would become so important in my life.

In my fourth year in Tijuana, it must have been 1999, I was already 19, almost twenty. By then, my work had evolved to managing the bar, including special services, though I still handled the difficult tasks—collections and the recovery of merchandise. I enjoyed my work; I knew I was good at it. I had saved up money from the "extraordinary" services I had performed, even bought some books, a TV, and a video game. Marín used to say in his letters that I needed to buy books to learn something.

Wally was an avid reader, something rare in a world like ours. Back then, he was my role model, and I thought that if he had risen so high with the boss's jobs, it must have been because he read and understood abstract concepts. I wanted to be like him, and I assured myself I could be. I followed his example, dedicating some hours to reading Jules Verne. They told me I had to understand Dante's verses, and even though sometimes my effort exceeded the results, I didn't give up.

One afternoon, while pretending to read—since I wasn't very good at it—and lying on my cot, a group of the "pigeon ladies" (what we called the prostitutes in our building) came to the office on the ground floor, most of them shouting and crying. Wally attended to them and only a second later, shouted for me, pulling me from what little concentration I had left.

He warned me of the situation: Yamila had been "picked up," and there was little information on how to find her. All we knew was that she had been taken in a 1969 Chevrolet Malibu, orange in color. As strange as it seemed, this combination of car and model was quite common in the '90s in Tijuana. Wally told me I'd be well paid if I found her, and that I could even take a vacation if I succeeded in completing this new mission. I didn't hesitate, and in no time, I was on the job.

Minutes later, I was driving the RAM truck, scanning the graffiti-covered streets of the hills in Tijuana. I crossed the narrow streets of Lomas Taurinas, trying to focus all my energy on finding the target. I figured we would find the orange car in the poorer neighborhoods; we'd be sure of it, if only we knew if the plates were Mexican. As I drove, my gun between my legs for quick access, I craned my neck, my eyes straining as if I could somehow speed up the process.

Out of nowhere, and to my luck, the described vehicle appeared before my eyes. I saw people struggling in the back, and through the rear window, I could make out Yamila's legs—whom I still only referred to as "the Southern girl." I decided to act fast, pulled ahead of the car, and cut it off with the truck. The driver swerved onto the sidewalk, knocking over a newsstand. I knew it wouldn't be easy to stop him. The bright orange Malibu accelerated, ran a red light heading downtown, and tried to escape by turning right.

The chase lasted several minutes, through the steep streets around Tijuana. It wasn't until the intersection of Enrique González and Días Mirón that I saw my chance to ram the car with the truck, which I did. The car got wedged between the wall and my vehicle. I knew it was trapped and couldn't go any further, and confirmed it when the driver opened the door. The Malibu's windows were tinted, which made it difficult to see clearly. I thought he might be getting a weapon ready to fight back.

An instant later, the driver stepped out from the side of the car and shot at me with a silver revolver. Immediately, I threw myself to the floor of the truck, as I had already anticipated something like this could happen. Nervous and with my pulse racing, I searched for my weapon, which had fallen near the pedals of my vehicle. After some frantic moments, I found it, grabbed it tightly, and waited for a few seconds. Then, the passenger door of the truck opened, and I fired directly. As I shot, I leaped out of the vehicle with all my strength, and through the vehicle's undercarriage, I saw the man who had shot at me lying on the ground. A large pool of blood surrounded him. I took his weapon and stealthily climbed out of the truck.

The second man was getting out of the car, Yamila gripped tightly by the neck, but as he did, he hadn't heard the three shots fired from my Glock, as it had been modified with a suppressor, using parts from a Colt. The silencer, combined with subsonic ammunition — a tip from the bar's manager — made the shots nearly silent. The man shouted a name, which I couldn't fully understand, but I assumed it was the name of the one I had just killed. I quickly approached, as both of them had their backs turned. I pointed the gun at the man and ordered him to let her go. The fool couldn't have been more than sixteen, and almost instinctively, he yelled to his companion again. The other didn't respond. I told him to turn slowly, and there, lying on the floor in the middle of the bloodstain, he saw his dead friend.

"This is how crimes are paid for, my friend," I said, "these are blood debts." The man stood still, his pale face betraying his fear of the inevitable, as he knew exactly where I stood.

"Do it now!" he yelled after a few moments.

I refused. I knew he would beg another time — something about the situation made me think so. Instead, I shot him in the knee, marking him for life. Now, he would remember who Pasa was.

I grabbed Yamila by the arm and pulled her into my vehicle, quickly driving away, struggling to get clear of the man crushed between the wall and my truck. As I looked at the windshield, I saw five bullet holes. I sped away from the scene as fast as I could. In the distance, I could hear the wail of sirens from patrol cars and ambulances, while people gathered around the corpse, some attempting to help the man I had shot in the knee.

Deep down, I felt a sense of pride for how well I had handled things. But moments later, when a red light stopped me in my tracks, the woman sitting beside me unexpectedly launched herself at me, fists flying. I couldn't believe it — after all I'd done to save her from her captors, now she was attacking me. I had barely managed to get her out of harm's way, and I had saved her life, but instead of gratitude, this was the reaction I got. I struggled to hold her back, steering the vehicle with one arm as she continued to scream at me, curse me, and hurl insults my way.

At first, she scolded me for nearly killing her by crashing into the car she was in. I excused myself, explaining that otherwise, they wouldn't have stopped. Between tears and fury, she told me that's exactly what she had wanted — for no one to have been able to stop her escape. Then, she accused me of being a disgusting pervert, someone who only looks but never acts. I was stunned. I didn't know how to respond. She went on, telling me that someday, I would want to escape too, and they would stop me — that I deserved it for bringing her back to that hellhole "Jake Mate." But most of all, she berated me for not being able to do anything against her, calling me the privileged nephew of the Uncle, and accusing me of being too scared to take out Wally. She believed I didn't act because I was a coward, a "wet blanket," and had the impression that I was a closet homosexual who was disgusted by people like her.

"A normal guy can't take so many insinuations without reacting," she spat, "and you, you don't even respond, you don't even turn to look." She paused, her voice dripping with malice before she continued: "It's obvious you don't like women. You must have something with that fag Wally, that's why you admire him and follow him to the death." Through sobs, she added, "You should just kill me. You're such an idiot, you've pushed me to the limit. If you kill me now, everything ends — it'll be good for me, and for you too."

When we finally arrived at "Jake Mate," I couldn't avoid a few of her kicks, slaps, and punches in my back as I carried her to the office of Wally. Once we were inside the small two-by-three-meter room, she stopped hitting me. She asked, gently this time, for me to let her walk on her own. She adjusted her floral dress and looked me in the eyes. Then, as if the furious woman who had cursed me all the way here was someone else entirely, she simply said:

"Thank you, Pasa. You're the most handsome, attractive, and sweet guy I've ever met." She smiled and then turned to Wally, telling him, "He saved my life. I owe it to him to be here with you, safe and sound."

"Yes, Sureña, Pasa is a good gunslinger. He's brave, and he's not as foolish as some might think... not in the Mexican sense, at least," Wally said, glancing at me as he continued. "You know, I have to admit... I was wrong about you, Pasa," Wally said, his eyes fixed on me. "You're the best, without a doubt. I'm completely sure you'll go far. You'll do it through your hard work, and with my protection—and the old man's too."

I couldn't speak a word. My lips were dry, and my throat felt like it was locked up, as if there was a stake lodged in it, preventing me from talking. I simply nodded and raised my eyebrows, struggling to swallow, hoping to get some saliva down. I retreated to my room and locked myself in. For the first time since I had started down this rough path, I genuinely doubted whether it was a good idea to stay in this line of work. I even began to question who I really was, and what kept me here. In the short time it took to return from that street corner to my place, something had shifted in me so deeply that I felt awful about myself. I wanted to leave it all behind.

My whole belief system had collapsed. Now, I wasn't sure if following Wally was a good idea. I wanted answers but had no idea what any of this meant anymore. I thought about drastically changing my course, but I had no foundation to make that happen. I also wondered if I should tell Marín about all these doubts that had been plaguing my mind.

For the past few days, whenever Yamila saw me, she muttered some words under her breath, giving me looks of contempt. The women around her did the same, and their stares made me feel small and miserable. They made me uncomfortable. I decided to ask Wally to change my sleeping arrangement. I wouldn't offer an explanation; I'd just say I wanted a change, and I wasn't lying. When I told the manager of "Jake Mate" that I wanted to move rooms, he looked at me and, with genuine disdain, told me I wasn't in a hotel and had no right to ask for a change. He said that while I was fulfilling my duties, I wasn't doing anything extraordinary. In the end, he hesitated and asked me why I wanted to move. I told him I was bored of the place, and since there were probably going to be more debt-collection jobs in the coming months, I thought it would be better to be downstairs where things might be busier. He looked at me and said, "You want something more than just collecting debts. I don't know what it is, but it's probably about Yamila. Whatever it is, trust me, it's fine. If you do it, I won't charge you for it," he said, changing the subject and rejecting my request to move.

I didn't know what to do. Something was pushing me to behave differently toward her. I liked her, but I knew I shouldn't get closer. Still, Wally's words echoed in my head: *"If you do it, I won't charge you for it."* Every time I repeated them, I felt disgusted with him—and with myself. I realized that I had done nothing good for that little woman with sky-blue eyes. My thoughts tangled whenever I considered them, though I'd always known that what I was doing was just work. Now, I wasn't sure how professional it really was.

I had always convinced myself that I didn't need anything more in life—nothing beyond Marín's protection and Wally's orders. But a part of me had changed. I didn't want to continue this anymore.

On Mondays, my day off, I usually planned to go find some distractions. I had made up my mind to head toward the border and find something to entertain myself with. Wally, who had noticed I was troubled after rescuing Yamila, asked me to come to his office. He told me to close the door behind me. He sat at his desk and, as usual, rummaged through the drawers of the metal filing cabinet, pulling out a bag with a significant amount of dollars. He handed it to me and said, "If you want to take someone for a vacation, you can. I can even give you one of the vehicles we have outside," referring to the trucks used for transporting goods.

I took the money in silence, looked into the man's eyes as he handed it to me, and sighed, like a wounded bull. Before I could say anything, he spoke first.

"You're quiet, chilango. That's not like you. What's going on?" he asked, pulling out a bottle of Macallan from the back, pouring the whiskey into a red cup. Then, he blew into a white cup with a logo I couldn't quite remember, filling it with alcohol too, and handed it to me. "It's that Argentine girl, isn't it? She's driving you crazy."

"Yeah," I breathed deeply, relieved to confess it, but couldn't bring myself to say anything else.

"It happens to all of us, chilanguillo," he said, drinking almost all the contents of the red cup in one gulp. "Listen, I'll make you a deal. Take her, do whatever you want with her. She's yours. If those idiots had taken her, it wouldn't have mattered. She's yours for a week, two weeks, whatever. There's no problem with that. I'm just worried about you. It's not good for the rest of us to see you so down, so distracted. You look sick, you damn chilanguillo."

Here's the translated and revised version of your text, maintaining its original structure while improving clarity and flow:

- Wally, what would you think if I told you I want to leave this behind? - I said boldly. - I've been thinking about it a lot.

- Well, that's bad, it's worse than I thought, - he said, pouring another generous shot of whiskey into my cup while also filling mine. - You shouldn't even be thinking about that, chilanguillo. The business is the business... you know, here you're valued, cared for, fed, hell, I'm even offering you women. Here, I'm like an older brother to you, but out there, no one's gonna care for you the way I do here. Stop messing around, your problem is that you think too much, that you're starting to believe you're better than you really are, that's your damn problem, I've always tried to show you that. - He paused and took a large gulp of his drink, setting the cup on the desk and staring at it as if searching for something. - Life passes, it's like a damn bottle of whiskey. One minute, it's full, and you think it'll always stay that way. You think you're invincible, that you can keep it full, happy, like you can take on the whole damn world. But just like that, everything ends, it breaks down; understand this, chilanguillo, you're fine here, you're safe.

- I get it, Wally, but...

- But nothing, you damn fool, are you a slow learner or something? - he interrupted me with a thick northern accent. - Look, stop with the nonsense, just keep going like you are. Go on vacation, take the Sureña with you, fuck her as much as you want, come back in three weeks, and you'll be as happy as you are today.

- I don't want to go on vacation, I want to keep working like I've been doing, - I said sincerely. - But how about I think about the whole Yamila thing?

- There you go, that's how you need to think, stop with the bullshit that's gonna cost you more in the end. - He poured more Macallan into my cup and filled mine again. - Let's toast, because, after all, you always show me you're not as dumb as I think you are. - We both raised our cups, clinked them together, and drank the whisky, which had an exquisite taste.

Since that moment and in the following weeks, I kept wondering what I wanted out of life. I didn't have many answers, since I knew so little and had always been tied to this... the "business"... collecting debts, hurting people, killing, kidnapping, intimidating — that was it. But deep inside, I knew something, I didn't want to separate from her. She deserved something better than this mess. I thought I could do better, clear my name, do something else... but that's when the problems came. I didn't know how to do anything else, but surely, I could learn.

Every night, as she went to dance at "Jake Mate," I'd sneak to one of the tables and watch her, trying not to be seen. I imagined her getting away from all this, with me. I closely observed her figure, liking her slightly toned legs, her flat stomach that gently curved near her pelvis. I loved the rosy hue of her skin, not pale like the others. Her large, almond-shaped eyes, mysterious breasts, the way she moved rhythmically — her hips swaying without being exaggerated like the others she danced with.

Although I liked watching her, something about entering the "Jake Mate" to see her bothered me. It was when a man touched her, when they approached and slipped bills into her underwear. Part of me would boil with rage, I'd lose control, sick with jealousy. I would leave quickly, wondering how I had let it get to this point. When she finished her long shifts, she'd sometimes come upstairs exhausted, other times crying. And when that happened, my feelings became even more confused. Still, I avoided speaking to her, even dodging her gaze if it met mine.

I had always thought my work was easy, that I was good at it. There were no complications. There was nothing to worry about other than the tight bond between my gun and me. I even began to think that every time I had to use my pistol, it was for something positive, like some kind of avenger. Perhaps it was a lingering feeling from when I killed Gato, or maybe it was just a justification for starting this life and having no way out. That's what I thought when the Sureña turned her back on me, when she refused to eat at the same table or when she gave me that look of disdain that only she could carry to such extremes.

Her contempt for me grew stronger and stronger, until one night, just before she went out to dance, I intercepted her on the iron stairs. I grabbed her by the waist and pressed her against my body, carrying her back toward our quarters. She resisted, tried to scream, kick me, even tried to use her elbows to hit me, but I was used to struggling with people four times her size and at least a head taller.

I covered her mouth with my hand and told her to listen carefully, assuring her I wasn't going to hurt her. I asked in a demanding tone:

- So, you want to leave, don't you, Sureña? You want to go... well, let's go then. - I said firmly, very close to her ear. I had to repeat it two or three times, as the panic attack I had caused made it hard for her to understand. She writhed like a worm, and I held her tighter, until I overpowered her and pushed her into my room.

Let me tell you something, I whispered in her ear as I pressed her against me, holding her against the wall:

- I'll help you get out of this shitty life. I'll do it as long as you come with me, because I really care about you. I don't know what I feel when you're near me. I really want to help you, if you stop screaming and promise not to tell anyone, we can plan this together.

She looked at me with her sky-blue eyes and nodded.

- I thought you were going to kill me, - she said, scared. - I thought the girls had told Wally I wanted to escape, and he was going to have me executed. That's why I was ready to leave it all behind, just to get out alive. Forgive me, pibe.

- Carmelo doesn't know anything... - For the first time since I arrived in Tijuana, I dared to say Wally's real name. I said it while checking to see if anyone was behind the door, listening. - I won't tell him, I understand you want to escape, that you're not made for all this crap, that you deserve something better. That's why I want to ask you to run away with me. You and I can start a new life, just the two of us, without Carmelo, without the Tío, without Jake Mate, without clients, without deaths, none of this bullshit.

She smiled and then said...

- I don't know who this Carmelo is, but that last part was really sweet, and I think it could work. I think we could start over. I've always dreamed of doing something different from all this.

I told her Carmelo Pérez was Wally's real name, that even though I didn't know much, I could learn. I could become a mechanic or try to get a job somewhere else. I confessed she inspired me to be a better man. She looked at me with eyes like no one had ever looked at me before, or maybe it was just my mother, but it had been so long since anyone had looked at me like that. With a tenderness that caressed, with an inexplicable interest, as if nothing else in the world mattered. Then she kissed me gently, placed her hand on my forehead, and said, "I'll go to the ends of the earth if that's what you want."

Without warning, she hurried out of my room. I impulsively followed her. When she stepped out, I noticed she adjusted her bra, while Wally watched her from below. When I followed her, he saw me from a distance, raised his eyebrows, shook his head from side to side, and smiled at me.

For a few hours, doubt crept into my mind. Perhaps it hadn't been a good idea to tell her Wally's real name or to reveal my intentions with her. After all, I was the only one who knew it. Still, I saw it as a gesture of mutual trust. Yet, I couldn't shake the worry that Wally might have noticed something unusual after seeing Yamila leave my room. I decided to clear my doubts. In the early hours of the morning, when the bar was nearly empty, I found Carmelo Pérez, a few drinks too deep. I looked him in the eyes, trying to read him, to find some clue about what he thought of me. He spoke with some difficulty, slurring his words due to the heavy amount of alcohol he had consumed that night.

"You're something else, Pasa. I never saw it coming... Look at you—all scrawny, but a damn stud," he said, a crooked grin spreading across his face. "You left her wrecked, poor girl. She even asked for permission to leave early—said she was too tired. That damn Sureña."

"She told you, didn't she?" I hesitated to press further.

"Yeah, said you had her before her shift even started. And I've already told you—it's fine," he muttered before burping. "You planning to take her away for a while or what?"

"Yes, Wally, that's what I wanted to talk to you about," I replied firmly.

"It's fine by me," he said with finality.

And so, Yamila and I fled Tijuana and our shared history at the "Jake Mate" one July night in 1999. Our destination was Cancún—a place where we hoped to start anew. More importantly, it was as far away as possible from Wally and Marín. We traveled overland, stopping in every town and city along the way. During that journey, my life changed completely. Whether for better or worse, I'm still not sure.

12. CISEN Data Processing Center, Mexico City. 5:15 PM, July 30th.

Alejandro Harlington arrived at the facility. He was escorted through the main parking lot and took the elevator reserved for executives. As he walked, a text message buzzed on his phone. It read: "**THERE ARE LEADS**." Two military personnel escorted him, while several civilian workers exchanged glances, greeted him, and extended their hands. He was informed that all regional security commissioners, several directors, and four high-ranking officials were gathered in one of the second-floor meeting rooms.

As Harlington entered the room, the attendees stood in acknowledgment. He mentally rehearsed what he was about to say. The crux of his speech was simple: *he was no fool, and he needed tangible results within the next few hours.* Five hours had passed since the kidnapping, and no concrete leads had surfaced. *"We are not the laughingstock of the nation,"* he repeated to himself, almost as a mantra, trying to internalize it.

He positioned himself in front of the semicircle of chairs and addressed them with clarity:

"Gentlemen, this has been a long and uncomfortable afternoon—one of those we never want to face in public service. However, the events that unfolded at noon today have put us to the test.

In the hours since, I have witnessed the tireless efforts of my team, and I know you have worked just as hard. But it hasn't been enough. As of this moment, we still have no knowledge of Mr. Pérez Brito's whereabouts.

This is a challenging moment, and I must ask for just a bit more from each of you. I understand that my moral authority to make such a request is limited, but I need to make it nonetheless.

I spoke personally with President Trevilla just hours ago. He has made it clear: we must locate the father of Senator Pérez Irigoyen—*at any cost.*

So, I want to hear your ideas. Believe me, at this point, any opinion is valuable and will be taken with the seriousness it deserves.

We will spare no resources, and we will not stop, but we must remain focused. Let's review what we know so far.

Thank you for your efforts."

One of the women in the room picked up a laser pointer, and a series of slides appeared on various screens mounted around the walls. The slides displayed photographs of the incident: bullet trajectories, the bridge, the lanes of the Periférico, the bullets themselves, and the marks they had left on the asphalt. She presented the technical details, but while her words echoed in his ears, Harlington's mind was elsewhere.

He replayed a conversation he'd had with Francisco Leyva, a former soldier who had been involved in numerous armed conflicts across Mexico over the past twenty years. Leyva had told him that this incident bore the hallmark of someone highly skilled with weapons and hungry for publicity. Years earlier, Leyva had seen something similar in Monterrey, orchestrated by *"El Tío*"—a military officer expelled from the armed forces after several controversies, including involvement in drug trafficking.

Leyva had said, *Look, Alejandro, I'm too old to be chasing shadows,*" *but you should start looking for this 'Tío.' What I can tell you with absolute certainty is that this kidnapping wasn't random. They knew which vehicle their target was in, they knew there were two passengers, and they knew the Lincoln wasn't being driven by the one they were after. They understood the origin of the journey and likely the destination too. Considering it would've been much easier to kidnap someone in a near-empty parking lot or at a traffic light, they chose instead to do it in "full view of everyone. This is terrorism in its purest form*

Harlington felt the pieces clicking into place and decided to ask:

"General Leyva, do you think this is political?" he asked hesitantly. "Because I can't find any other connection."

"It must be," the old soldier replied with certainty. "But the one who stands to benefit the most is the victim's son. Think about it, Harlington—why would it have to be so public? This is a publicity stunt. So, between you and me, you'll find him alive."

"You mentioned the similar incident in Monterrey," Harlington pressed. "Do you happen to recall the name of this 'Tío'?"

"Marín. Guillermo Marín, Brigadier General," the elder answered definitively.

"Thank you, General Leyva. It's always a pleasure talking with you."

"You should talk to me more often, Alejandro." The man stood up from the table at *Le Moustache* and walked out.

The National Security Commissioner's mind snapped back to the meeting room. He glanced around at the others present: some were jotting down notes, others sketching diagrams, and a few fidgeting with their pens. Long faces were the only common feature among all attendees. The presentation by the woman in the ill-fitting blue suit had concluded. Moments later, Harlington's secretary burst into the room, apologized for the interruption, and informed the Commissioner that the information he had requested was ready. Addressing the group, he began:

"Gentlemen, after my meeting with President Trevilla, I decided to reach out to some of the informants the Mexican government has relied upon over the past two decades. One of them, whom I will refer to as 'FL,' is a protected witness. He has provided us with the following details.

Twenty years ago, in Monterrey, Nuevo León, Colonel Ignacio Santibañez, a key figure in the fight against one of the dominant cartels in the northern region of the country, was kidnapped. Responsibility for the act was later claimed by a paramilitary group known as *La'*

'Barra or *'La Organización'* led by 'El Tío'—the alias of former General Guillermo Marín."

As he spoke, images of the kidnapping, sourced from a local newspaper from the late 1990s, appeared on the screens. One showed a black-and-white photo of the victim, dressed in a checkered suit, a stocky man with a dark complexion. Another displayed an image of a man in military uniform: a closely cropped haircut, a straight nose, and a full beard, his expression radiating toughness.

The slides transitioned to images of the Monterrey kidnapping scene, depicting a car on the side of a highway with a bullet hole in its windshield. From this vehicle, Colonel Santibañez had been forcibly taken. He was held captive for 23 days before being executed. His body was discovered eight years later in a clandestine grave in Cadereyta.

The attack was used as a form of local propaganda—more than a kidnapping, it was an act of terrorism. At the time, most people were aware that 'El Tío' controlled human trafficking operations from Baja California to Coahuila, along with drug distribution, including marijuana and opium poppies. Over time, Marín and his network expanded their operations to include large quantities of synthetic drugs and acids, adapting to the shifting landscape of the narcotics trade."

- *El Tío*, that is, General Guillermo Marín, was captured a few years ago. He is currently serving a sentence for health-related crimes, criminal conspiracy, human trafficking, drug trafficking, conspiracy, kidnapping, and possession of military-grade weapons. He is incarcerated at the Altiplano Social Reintegration Center in Almoloya de Juárez, State of Mexico. I contacted the prison director, who confirmed that, like many other inmates there, Marín enjoys certain special privileges. For years, he has been held in isolation from the general prison population. Among his privileges is a collection of items in his cell, which, at least officially, do not include any telecommunications devices.

At this point, this is the most consistent information we have. However, I ask that it remains confidential within this room. It is still too early to categorize this incident as an act of terrorism or to confirm Marín's direct involvement. What we can assert, however, is that the kidnapping was no random event. Its characteristics strongly suggest it was carried out as a propagandistic act, rather than a simple ransom operation.

- Dr. Harlington, - interrupted a man in a black suit with a white shirt and a blue-and-white striped tie. - If this individual, General... Marín, - he said after checking his notes - is implicated, it would mean we have a paramilitary group targeting a presidential *de facto* candidate. This complicates matters further, as electoral legislation requires us to cooperate with the electoral crimes prosecutor's office.

- Or, that's what they want us to believe, Analyst Fernández, - Dr. Harlington interjected, gesturing with his hand for the man to pause. - What I need from you all is to investigate every possible ramification of the criminal organization Marín led two decades ago. This will not be an easy task. However, I believe we can gain time, and I assure you that if this theory—currently our only plausible one—is correct, we will find Mr. Raúl Pérez alive. Let me remind you that whoever orchestrated this kidnapping knew the origin and destination of the victim's journey, the exact schedule of their route, and likely had a connection with the victim's driver. I need to know who the informant might have been.

- What will the Mayor declare during the press conference in less than an hour? - asked another man dressed in a black suit and matching shirt.

- That is not for us to determine, Mr. Gómez. What we need is to identify the perpetrators. There is a possibility that the President will address the nation at 9:00 PM—a move I have consistently opposed. However, I doubt I can influence the right individuals to prevent such remarks or ensure that the President's political advisors guide him to avoid making premature statements about the "investigation."

The staff got to work, fully aware that it would be a long night. Dr. Harlington rose from his seat, adjusted his jacket, and buttoned it. He once again thanked everyone for their efforts and assured them that their dedication would be recognized.

While President Trevilla and some of his advisors were eager to shape public opinion, Harlington had requested a discreet and intelligent handling of the situation. A phone call confirmed that his recommendations had been heeded. The President would limit his 9:00 PM address to highlighting the investments made in security and the fight against organized crime.

Alejandro Harlington also knew that there was a significant chance that one of the generals who had served the nation during the 1990s might know something. He instructed two analysts to compile a list of the primary leaders of the northern military zones of the country. He suspected that perhaps one of Marín's former associates, still at large, might have taken control of his organization. It even crossed his mind that the left-wing factions, which had always been reactionary, might have commissioned someone to get rid of Pérez Irigoyen.

He tried not to dwell too much on the possibility but wondered if Mayor Márquez had provided certain *facilitations* to someone. Perhaps one of his close associates had intellectually masterminded the plan alongside a professional—a provocateur. It would require someone bold, someone who had motives to show off in this way. Harlington tasked another group of analysts to gather information on the top marksmen within the Mexico City Police Department. Was there someone skilled enough to create this level of chaos with a single bullet?

As each team reported their findings, provided data, and reviewed lines of investigation in a somewhat logical order, Harlington observed and engaged with each of them. He meticulously went through every piece of information they brought, reviewing each parameter alongside his team. Meanwhile, the words he had spoken to his assistant earlier echoed in his mind: *"We are intelligence, Luis Roberto. We aren't stupid enough to overlook something of this magnitude."*

Nobody kidnaps an important figure in broad daylight. Nobody defies the government's authority in such a brazen way—at least, not someone who isn't entirely unhinged. He felt that something had slipped past him, but he couldn't pinpoint what. *Someone is playing us, mocking us. That damned bastard wants to ruin us.* The mere thought of admitting this filled him with both anger and doubt. Yet doubt was a luxury he could neither afford nor permit—especially not against an unknown enemy, a ghost, a total maniac bent on destruction.

Analyst Fernández informed him over the phone that General Aragón, an old friend of Dr. Harlington, was on the line with additional information. Aragón claimed to have evidence suggesting that the incident had been orchestrated by a group of broadband concessionaires. These businessmen, significantly impacted by Senator Pérez Irigoyen's reform, might have kidnapped his father as leverage to prevent losing the broadband frequency set to be auctioned by the Federal Government's Electricity Production Commission.

Harlington took the call and listened carefully to General Aragón's arguments. However, something didn't sit well with him. Instead of following that line of inquiry, he decided to shift focus.

"General Aragón, I appreciate the information you've provided. However, the course of events has already taken another direction," Harlington said sincerely.

"There's no need to thank me, Doctor. It's my patriotic duty," Aragón replied, a hint of mischief in his tone. "I'd like to know which line of investigation you're pursuing."

- "Do you know General Guillermo Marín?" Harlington asked bluntly.

- "A more precise question would be, 'Who doesn't know Marín?'" General Aragón replied with a wry smile. "That madman is definitely involved... It wouldn't surprise me."

- "Why do you know him, sir? Have you met him in person?" Harlington asked, full of doubt.

- "Yes, he was my brother-in-arms on several occasions. Let's just say I had the chance to spend a few nights at different events with him. He was the commander of the northern zone during the era of Humberto Salgado, the *Czar*," Aragón paused for a moment. "I think it was in the mid-'80s that I spent the most time with Marín."

- "Would you be willing to come with me to see him?" Harlington asked without thinking too much. "I believe that man knows something we don't."

- "Serving my country is the only goal I have in life, Doctor. If you want me to accompany you, I'll gladly do so," the General replied firmly. "But let me warn you, it won't be a pleasant encounter. That man certainly knows how to get under people's skin."

- "I'll be waiting for you at the Data Processing Center on Constituyentes in twenty minutes," Harlington said. "I won't say goodbye, General."

- "I'll see you there, Doctor."

Harlington immediately ordered the drafting of an official document to assign Javier Aragón a provisional role, which he personally approved. The arrival of the General boosted his confidence. He picked up the phone in the data processing room and requested the contact number for the Altiplano prison. Turning to his subordinates, he stated that he believed this was where they could begin investigating the whereabouts of Engineer Raúl Pérez.

Soon after, Aragón entered the data room, escorted by two soldiers. Without hesitation, Harlington said they needed to catch Marín off guard. If the man was involved, he wouldn't be able to withstand the pressure of losing control of the situation.

The older man, with a long beard, muttered some words that made no sense to those seated at the desks. However, something caused Harlington to reassess his doubts. He took a deep breath and stated they would need a contact within the Senate itself, as that's where a thorough investigation should begin. Yet he also acknowledged that such a move would be illegal due to the constitutional immunity of senators.

- "General Aragón, do you honestly believe there are senators involved?" Harlington asked sincerely. "If that's the case, we can set up a network of informants. There's intelligence personnel in every corridor of both chambers."

- "You shouldn't lose sight of that possibility, Doctor Harlington," the older man replied calmly. "Why don't you commission someone to gather information about the meetings Senator Pérez Irigoyen has held, particularly with leftist groups?"

- "It seems we'll need to shift roles and responsibilities. I'll assign Gómez and Fernández to investigate an informant's sources within the Senate," Harlington said, trying to organize his thoughts. "I'd also like to examine the relationship between Márquez and the Senator," he concluded, referring to the Mayor.

Aragón suggested that the wisest course of action would be to wait for another call from the captors. He somberly reminded them that protocol dictated it was a bad sign that no one had called back after so many hours. It was possible the captive was either dead or severely injured, and without medical attention, survival was unlikely. Given the victim's advanced age, the likelihood of survival was drastically reduced. Aragón noted that such delays were common in kidnappings where the victim's condition was critical.

He also argued that when events began as violently as they had in this case, approximately seventy-five percent of hostages ended up dead. This meant that, in the absence of a phone call, they would have to start considering the possibility of a corpse. That information deeply affected Harlington.

"Perhaps the hostage recognized his captors," Aragón suggested. "Or maybe something went wrong during the transfer, and they were forced to dispose of him. It's just a possibility," the elderly man with the long white beard said in a somber tone. "Not a certainty."

Alejandro Harlington made a slight motion with his mouth, a gesture of acceptance, though Aragón's words had only unsettled him in ways he hadn't anticipated. A wave of disappointment and uncertainty swept over him, leaving him with a gnawing feeling that nothing was going as it should.

The Commissioner stepped out of the facility for a moment and stood by a grassy field. He retrieved a cigarette from the pack in his jacket's inner pocket, alongside the photographs taken by the Technological Institute's camera—the last ones the device had captured.

No one else had seen those photos, or at least, no one who was privy to intelligence matters. For reasons unknown, he slipped them back into his jacket and smoked the cigarette in almost a single exhale. Aragón caught up to him and asked for one as well. Harlington handed him the pack and offered a light.

"I wouldn't want to be in your shoes," the older man remarked.

Harlington merely raised his eyebrows and admitted that in twenty-five minutes, a helicopter would take him and other high-ranking officials to Altiplano. He asked Aragón for advice on how to handle Marín.

The elder placed his left hand—his free hand—on his head, running it over his sparse, graying hair. He took a deep breath, clicked his tongue, and locked eyes with Harlington.

"Surprise him, Commissioner," he advised. "Marín is a man who thrives on control, which is why he commands so much respect. He's a tough nut to crack, a provocateur, a braggart. He loves holding all the cards. His life has been all about creating chaos and instability. To put it simply, he's spent his life being both the problem and the solution. That's why he's so feared."

Their conversation was interrupted by a ringing phone. The screen of Harlington's mobile displayed the word *"Presidency"* Without hesitation, he redirected the call.

Harlington knew that President Trevilla's advisors had already spoken to him. The high-profile nature of the kidnapping jeopardized the country's stability, raising doubts about the government's ability to resolve an issue that threatened public security on an unprecedented scale.

At that moment, the public was asking themselves: *If someone as important and politically significant as Pérez Brito could be kidnapped without hesitation, what could happen to me?*

The collective anxiety was fueled by 24-hour news channels, which repeatedly broadcasted archive footage from the morning and provided hourly updates on how the abduction had occurred on the bustling Periférico highway. This only amplified the growing tension.

On another front, Pérez Irigoyen's powerful position in the Senate made the situation even more delicate and politically unstable. The public wanted the President to appear with Pérez Brito alive and in his arms.

Harlington wanted to make a public statement but, more importantly, to apprehend a suspect, handcuffed and ready to be delivered to the Federal Judiciary. There were too many moving parts in the political puzzle, and very little within anyone's grasp.

The image and political advisors of Fidel Trevilla advised him to deliver another nationally broadcasted message. However, the more radical ones suggested that instead of a prerecorded statement, he should invite journalists to Los Pinos for a live press conference with questions and answers. If such an event were called, all special coverage outlets would attend. Moreover, international agencies were pressuring for interviews with the President.

Another element at play was social media. On Twitter, the trending topic **#FindHimAlive** was the most replicated, while hashtags like **#IncompetentState** and **#NoJusticeMX** also gained significant traction. The public discourse revolved around insecurity and the motives behind Raúl Pérez Brito's abduction.

Adding to the tension, a state visit by six Latin American presidents was scheduled for just over a week later. This was in the context of signing a regional agreement for collaboration in the fight against drug trafficking. The U.S. President and the Canadian Prime Minister were among the honored guests. However, the widespread media frenzy, now reaching the most remote regions of the planet, severely jeopardized the President's and the country's efforts to project an image of a "safe Mexico" cultivated over the past five years.

Harlington had an ace up his sleeve. He intended to access the Senate's database, starting by reviewing the servers. This would include all electronic communications: phone calls, social media messages, emails, and security camera footage. Somewhere in this data, he believed they would find links to the political enemies of Senator Pérez Irigoyen. Gómez, a skilled hacker, was the ideal man for such an operation. Reentering the building, Harlington sought him out, leading him into one of the hallways connecting to the stairwell.

- *"Gómez, I need a favor, a personal one,"* Harlington muttered as he buttoned his jacket. *"I can trust you, right?"*

- *"Of course, Doctor. Tell me what you need."* Gómez responded, locking eyes with him.

- *"I want you to access the main Senate server. Extract every contact Senator Pérez Irigoyen has had with individuals who fit the profile of informants,"* the Commissioner stated firmly.

- *"Sir... but that's... illegal,"* Gómez replied hesitantly. *"The division of powers—"*

- *"I am well aware of the division of powers,"* Harlington interrupted, irritation evident in his tone. *"That's why I told you this is a personal favor."* He pulled out a pack of cigarettes almost mechanically. *"Favors, Gómez, are not always legal or procedural, but we are talking about human lives, damn it."*

- *"I'll do it, sir. It's just that... I thought perhaps you'd overlooked the legal aspect,"* Gómez stammered, trying to justify his hesitation.

- *"I want a report before midnight. Focus on individuals with criminal records, ties to organized crime, or connections to the armed forces,"* Harlington instructed firmly.

- *"Understood, sir,"* Gómez replied with a nod.

- *"One more thing. This stays between you and me. No one else can know about this special request."*

- *"You have my word, sir,"* Gómez assured him.

Harlington's phone buzzed again. The words "Presidency" appeared on the screen, sending a chill down his spine. He answered.

- *"What do you have for me, Alejandro? I trust we've had an update,"* President Trevilla began.

- *"I have some leads, but I'll need you to keep this between us,"* Harlington replied, trying to maintain his composure. *"We believe the culprit behind the abduction is someone named Guillermo Marín."*

- *"Marín? What the hell is his role in all of this?"* the President asked, bewildered. *"Are you certain, Doctor Harlington, that this is the right path forward?"*

- *"Yes, Mr. President,"* Harlington affirmed. *"I'm confident. Whoever is behind this is his enemy, sir."*

Harlington mentally refined his statement, realizing that the enemies in question weren't just foes of a single man but adversaries of an entire nation. The Senator's political or corporate rivals could have easily connected with any of Fernando's associates. These links might have gone unnoticed, except under the scrutiny of experts like Gómez, who would spend hours poring over computer screens. Meanwhile, Harlington hoped to uncover something swiftly.

During the call, Harlington sought the President's moral approval to take all necessary steps to find the perpetrator. He admitted to accessing the Senate's server, an act that violated the law and breached the separation of powers. Harlington explained briefly, but the President was unequivocal: they had to identify the culprit at any cost. Upon hearing the details, Trevilla insisted that Harlington proceed, even if it meant bending the rules.

The call ended without further complications. As Harlington approached the analysts again, his assistant suddenly entered to inform him that the helicopter to the Altiplano was ready at the building's helipad. There, they would meet the right man for a challenging task—a cunning figure who might hold critical information. Harlington instructed Aragón to accompany him, as they were about to visit a legend.

Maximum Security Prison of Altiplano, Almoloya de Juárez, State of Mexico, 5:23 PM, July 30th

In Cell 204, located in Block A, resides the inmate known by various aliases: Dagoberto Quesada Mendoza, Julión Mendiola Téllez, and Alberto Saravia Castro. However, his real name is Guillermo Marín. No one knows for certain how many more pseudonyms he has accumulated over his criminal history—rumor has it he has more aliases than days spent behind bars.

He was imprisoned in April 2004 by Federal Support Forces and sentenced to 65 years for the murder of 34 federal agents over a 12-year span. His charges also included the kidnapping of seven individuals, one of them an American, for which he was deemed the mastermind. Additionally, he faced accusations of drug trafficking and possession of weapons restricted to the military. At one point, he was nearly extradited to the United States but narrowly avoided it, much like he had escaped countless other close calls throughout his life.

Beyond the charges against him, including crimes against public health and other infractions, Marín claimed to be a politically persecuted criminal. He insisted that the accusations did not align with his actual offenses. He had attempted to file appeals multiple times, but if he ever had friends, they had long since abandoned him. The judge labeled him a cynical, psychopathic, and profoundly damaged man.

Few inmates have heard him speak in years; he rarely talks and mostly grunts. When he does communicate, it's often to curse. A problematic inmate, he has instigated two fights that almost escalated into full-blown riots.

Some prisoners call him *"180"* because he always turns his back on people, while others prefer *".The General"* Though he is a solitary figure in prison, stories circulate about his life before incarceration. It's said he was easygoing but lost his mind after being betrayed. Other inmates whisper about the "rank" he supposedly held in society, describing him as a man of influence who demanded reverence.

A rumor spread throughout the prison that his nickname is *The*“ ”.*Uncle*Speculation about the number of deaths attributed to him is rampant, though no one knows the actual figure. Marín never exercises, instead spending his days reading—although no one knows what kinds of books. His cell is packed with volumes, regularly replenished. Interrupting his reading is considered a dangerous act.

One day, in the prison yard, an inmate dared to joke about him, calling him “The Uncle.” Marín responded with nothing but a disdainful glare before lunging at the man. The instigator, a towering figure over six feet tall and weighing more than 500 pounds, was no match for Marín, who swiftly applied a chokehold, leaving him unconscious. This incident unfolded before the stunned eyes of dozens of inmates in the yard.

Dagoberto, as many call him, is said to be forty-nine years old. He spends between eight and ten hours a day exercising his mind inside his cell, under dim lighting, with his gaze fixed. His appearance is eerie, as it seems like his face is dripping through the long hair that falls from his head. He is an especially violent inmate. On another occasion, when he was out in the yard with his fellow prisoners, he bit one and nearly tore off his ear. His main pastime consists of hurling insults whenever someone approaches his cell. The scant twenty minutes he is allowed each week to leave his cell and go to the yard are avoided by everyone: no guards, no inmates, no one in their right mind approaches him. Everyone knows he is a consummate psychopath with no cure, and he takes pride in it. They also know one thing: he's a terrible person, but above all, intelligent. It’s said that he was very shrewd, one of those men who, without anyone’s support, grew to be one of the most feared in the country.

The prison director, a man well-versed in the system, believes that Marín's behavior is a result of his desire to be declared mentally unfit. However, whenever the inmate has requested such a diagnosis, the director personally fills out the forms to deny him that possibility. Deep down, Juan Carlos Meneses enjoys having a person like him behind the walls of his prison.

He was caught in Monterrey and accused and convicted of being the mastermind behind the clashes in which drugs, weapons, and twenty-two federal agents were killed, along with at least seven civilians. On his side, three hitmen fell that day. As the investigation advanced, he was accused of a long list of crimes. His lawyers managed to clear him of some charges, including human trafficking, because someone else took the blame, and others that were less notorious or ones no criminal of his caliber would ever accept. On the day of his capture, they found a shipment of four hundred kilos of cocaine. He was supposed to be confined in the Topo Chico prison, but due to some administrative reason, he was sent to the State of Mexico instead. Inside the prison, he had already been involved in several violent incidents. The ear incident was the most notorious and had given him enough fame to prevent anyone from bothering him. They say he chewed the ear for a few seconds, with some claiming he spat it out, while others swore he swallowed it. In the end, they all agreed that after finishing the gruesome act, he had stuck out his tongue and opened his mouth, which was full of blood dripping down his neck.

Another, less well-known incident occurred when a careless guard received a blow to the head that fractured his skull. The guard remained there, unconscious, until another officer noticed him. They say the blow caused severe damage to the neural circuits responsible for speech, and since then, the guard has been mute.

Since then, he's been kept in isolation, which wasn't the first time. In his youth, he loved terrorizing his classmates. As a child, he frequently played with everyone's mind, relishing the suffering of others, especially those who saw him as different, which he was. Back then, it was evident, but no one stopped him—who knows if they could have. Over time, he revealed himself as a cold, disciplined killer with exceptional mental strength. It was hard for him to lose focus, not that it made him extraordinary, but it allowed him to withstand nearly anything: isolation, poverty, misery, even illness. He had an uncanny resistance to disease. During the scarlet fever epidemic, which killed his only sister, he didn't even have a headache.

Now, he had let his hair and beard grow, both graying, neglected, and dirty, giving him a sometimes terrifying appearance. However, for others, it was easier to walk by him without suffering the scrutiny of his large, bright black eyes. The eyes, particularly their brightness, peeked through the tangled curtain of hair, occasionally revealing scars on his brown face and bushy, unkempt beard.

He often ate with his hands, despising the plastic utensils provided to him. His long, grimy nails adorned thin hands with chewed nails, inserted into fingers covered in hair. Deep down, he hated the prison food—it was always cold, mashed, and raw, salty, and lacked any aroma. Perhaps it was the food that made him miss his freedom, for he was always an unusually silent, calculating type. But sometimes, on rare occasions, he could be heard praying.

When he wasn't eating, he was turning the yellowed pages of his piled-up books. Sometimes, he could be heard reciting Hamlet's lines out loud, other times, murmuring poems by T.S. Eliot. But the most unsettling part came when a small, yellowish light would flicker on at 3:30 in the morning, followed by the sudden, loud laughter of the one occupying the isolation cell in Block A. Although no one in the prison knew exactly who was who, his readings were always combined into a repetitive logic, as if he were memorizing each paragraph. Sometimes, he would even realize he was muttering words, even nonsensical ones, in a mechanical tone. But that didn't matter; they were always for himself, for no one else.

There was a part of him deep down that knew something would happen, that one day, which was not far off, someone would make a mistake, some kind of miracle would set him free again. He couldn't imagine how, who, or why, but deep within himself, he knew, and that certainty was firmly rooted in him. It was somehow his anchor, the one thing he clung to in order not to lose his sanity entirely. He held on to a growing hope in his heart. Though he had adapted to the solitude of prison, he missed freedom and power—one was no good without the other. For him, it was enough to have that certainty, that knowledge that the day he was freed, he would also become the most powerful man in the nation.

Perhaps, without realizing it, he had thought about the possibility of escape. He imagined it happening one night when a distracted guard left his cell door open. Maybe a club would be enough to subdue him, to take a hostage, and with that, his freedom. But his mind's approach suggested that his true talents lay in intelligence and strategy, and it would be through these that he could confront the system, take revenge on those who had forgotten him, and those who had betrayed him—on every single one of them.

Meanwhile, each day, he focused on one simple idea: to escape that hell and watch everything he once knew burn to the ground. To exact revenge on those who had left him alone and abandoned like a dog, like a miserable wretch, in that place, thinking they could rot him, destroy him, kill him—and any other similar adjective. All the names of those who had locked him away, stored in his head, were repeated each night, and his hatred grew against each of the pigs he remembered.

Alejandro Harlington arrived by helicopter with his entourage, having accessed through the foul-smelling tunnel that separates the free men from the prisoners. As they walked, almost in the dark, with a nauseating feeling in the pit of their stomachs, the three men felt their hearts racing, while the stench of confinement gradually overtook their insides. Without warning, with each step, their doubts grew, accompanied by a sensation that was difficult to describe. At times, it felt like fear, and at other moments, it was violent, like the feeling of rage. The atmosphere had turned into a dense fog, and the sensation was as if it were closing in on them. With the shadows cast by the faint sodium vapor lights barely illuminating the nothingness, the mind becomes confused, distorted, and loses touch with reality. In the solitude of each man, one by one, new questions arose in their minds as they continued walking. Every obstacle took on a new paradigm of meaning.

At some point, the thunderous steps of the military were joined by another man escorting them—a prison guard, short in stature, with graying hair. At first, he gave them a brief, contemptuous glance, a common look among men hardened in this place. Without wasting time, he led them to where the prison director was already waiting for them.

General Zapata, the Attorney General, joined them. He had arrived by land just minutes before the Commissioner and his entourage. With military precision, he kept his pace steady. In his mind, he visualized the faces of his wife and three children. He wondered how he had gotten to this point, how it was possible that in weeks he hadn't heard anything from them. It was as though there were a force that kept him always distant from his family, absent. It felt like something he couldn't explain was keeping them apart, and deep down, the sensation was painful—not because it was unexplored, but because of what it would mean over time.

Zapata was a surprisingly sensitive man for someone chosen as the Attorney General. He had long been one of President Trevilla's weaknesses, often criticized as someone with insufficient abilities to hold the position for which he had been selected. Deep down, this towering figure had always feared being alone in life, and undoubtedly, what one fears most is exactly what life forces them to endure. When he looked at Alejandro Harlington and extended his hand, he was visibly exhausted. His footsteps echoed strangely hollow, and as Harlington approached him, he quietly thanked him for the support the Commission was receiving from him and his institution. Zapata, with a weary sigh, replied that they were in the same boat. Mechanically, he reached into the right pocket of his uniform pants where he always kept his cell phone, but it wasn't there. He'd left it at the security checkpoint of the prison. He sighed silently to himself.

He found himself wondering what trouble his youngest son, Arturo, was involved in, as he kept his head down and followed Harlington's steps. He knew Arturo had his problems—every teenager did—but he was aware that things had worsened in recent months. His debts were no secret, nor were the nights of partying and gambling. His credit card bills didn't match any legitimate expenses. Zapata sighed again and continued walking, wondering what was more important—his damned job that drained every ounce of energy from him or his family. Arguments had become a daily occurrence at home. He was also aware of Arturo's long absences from the Technological Institute, his bad grades, and the ones he bought at great cost. He resented himself for not knowing how to act or what to say. Perhaps that was why he had let the problem grow so much.

Life never gives you time to talk or change things; it just takes away what you love most, and the worst part is that the process is often radical, even swift, Zapata reprimanded himself. He removed his kepi and held it under his left arm, adopting the familiar posture of high-ranking military officers that with practice becomes second nature. Then, without thinking, he discreetly wiped the sweat from his forehead with the white handkerchief he always carried in the right rear pocket of his pants. The heat hit him hard, and beads of sweat ran uncomfortably down his forehead. He felt dizzy and nauseous, momentarily thinking he might choke.

When the guards asked for their identification, there was a brief pause for reflection. For some reason, his gaze again fell on his polished black shoes, now resting on the grimy, grease-streaked floor of the prison—grease that accumulated over time and was never cleaned. Again, his youngest son came to his mind: was he seeing someone, a woman? If so, why, and with what intentions? More importantly, would Arturo ever confide in him? Why was Arturo like this, not having inherited his discipline and ability to do things the right way? A rapid mental review flashed through his mind, followed by a sudden change in scenery. He imagined the chubby face of his eldest son, Salvador. A faint smile seemed to escape his lips, and that image provided him with a slight sense of calm.

In an instant, Zapata observed the stark differences between Arturo and Salvador. The latter, a polyglot devoted to his studies, had studied engineering just to please him. He was calm, often at home, and held the family's highest grades. In many ways, Salvador was his favorite son, filling him with immense pride, but also a deep sense of concern. Salvador's introversion, his misinterpretation of discipline, ultimately resulted in one painful truth: Salvador was insecure, slow, disorganized, and unable to quickly adapt to life's everyday challenges. Zapata knew he needed Salvador—his recommendations, his friends, his protection. Salvador was a different kind of man in every sense, and Zapata couldn't quite figure out whether he should view him as better or worse than Arturo.

He couldn't honestly say there was something he truly enjoyed doing. He was capable of studying, capable of learning, but beyond that, he lacked the ability to strategize and develop plans. His own introversion held him back from truly excelling. Perhaps he had been somewhat like that himself, but he had far surpassed it.

Could it be that the only thing he had focused on in his life was trying to buy my acceptance with cheap tricks? General Zapata repeated to himself mentally. He paused for a moment and realized how unfortunate it was that his son didn't know he loved him just the way he was, without needing to meet his or anyone else's expectations.

At Salvador's age, perhaps he hadn't known how to tell him that sometimes you have to stand up against life, the system, and the filth—and that you had to do it forcefully. He would have preferred that each of his children's abilities had been better utilized, but it was difficult, and in that moment, he felt responsible for everything. They moved on to Block A, eventually.

When they were finally allowed access to one of the long, winding hallways of the penitentiary, General Zapata sighed, feeling overwhelmed. Perhaps his breath had changed in volume, becoming audible. He paused mentally and tried once again to focus on something other than his family, but he couldn't. That feeling of confinement, and the cursed smell emanating from everywhere— from the walls, the floor, that rancid stench embedded in every cubic inch of air around him— consumed him.

He had to concentrate on the one thing that mattered right now: finding the victim of the Periférico Sur kidnapping. There was nothing else. He forced himself to focus. Yet, in a recess of his memory, what now played out in his mind were images like a continuous tape, battered by time, as if he were watching it in a shabby, old cinema. Perhaps he had sat there once, as a child, when his grandmother had taken him to watch a black-and-white movie, one of those where, if you looked closely at the screen, you could see countless imperfections. That was cinema in his time, he thought.

For some reason, after entering the prison, he had been unable to control the images coming to his mind. In them, he saw the faces of his daughter and wife. It had been a while since he had understood the behavior of either one of them. They were always distant. That was an impossible task to solve, and it wouldn't be worth spending any energy on it. Trying to clarify all their feelings wasn't an option, especially not now, when he was still dizzy and on the verge of collapsing at any moment, in the middle of a federal penitentiary where, by the way, when he had left his apartment on Prolongación Legaria that morning, he had never imagined he would end up there, feeling more trapped than many of the people serving sentences.

Now, everything around him felt so foreign and strange: the gray walls, the floors that had once been white but now were of an indescribable color. A sense of alienation overtook him. He breathed in, trying to ignore the rancid smell, and now, wandering through a fetid federal dungeon, he realized that he had wasted the majority of his life chasing ghosts, chasing nonexistent justice. In the end, he was left alone, overwhelmed by memories, and he secretly became frustrated. Life could change so quickly and radically, and as a result, anyone could have their life altered in just a few hours. For some reason he couldn't understand, he felt miserable, but he didn't tell anyone. He accepted it and kept moving forward.

Walking between the cells, where the filth of humanity took on the most profound meaning, with every step, the hollow sound of his shoes and those of his companions convinced him even more of the misfortune of the oppressed, who live and die in the daily oblivion of imprisonment. He knew that among all this scum, some didn't deserve to be there, but there was nothing to be done. As he continued, weighed down and silent, he looked carefully again and noticed the shape of the imprint left on the floor by his companions' shoes. It frustrated him—still smelling the conditions in which other human beings could live. It was then that he realized: it was life, the only thing he could have chosen, and he would have to live it in the best way possible, without needless anger. Once he left there, he would retire from the military for good and go somewhere far away, where that feeling would never find him.

The first wing of the high-security prison was inhabited, if the word could be used to describe those inside, by groups of petty criminals, with no chance of ever leaving. The cells were small, gray, greasy, and dirty, filled with earth and dust, the only companions of men who resigned themselves to dying slowly in confinement. The cells were covered with archaic drawings, sometimes resembling the cave paintings found on the walls of humanity's primal caves. Other times, they depicted abstract concepts from the minds of the incarcerated. In some instances, there were lines marked in groups of four, crossed by a fifth, to keep track of time—a unit of measure that had no value outside, but inside, it was the only form of time that existed.

That's what Harlington told him as he shared what he had been able to investigate. Without anyone caring, who's here and who's leaving, the one who stays falls into oblivion, and all that remains are those misshapen figures traced on concrete, with jagged edges distorting what they were meant to express.

They walked long enough to get lost in a complex labyrinth. They passed by other types of cells—some filled with madmen, others with powerful drug cartel bosses. The latter had cells filled with luxury—big TV screens, sound systems that played to alleviate the sadness of captivity with loud band and cumbia music. Some cells were of no importance, filled with wretched rags of men, long dead, forgotten by the world, and unadapted to prison life. Some moaned and sobbed, while others stared at the group with complete bewilderment. Many used their own feces to continue creating misshapen figures with shifting meanings on the prison walls.

At some point, the prison director joined them, offering countless apologies for the conditions in which the inmates lived, but in reality, no one had come to visit or to supervise the state of the institution. The only reason those men were walking those long, gray, and putrid hallways was because "El Tío" was inside, in one of those lost cells, in one whose number had never appeared in any report. Meneses led them to a space where the area was very quiet, and the walls appeared freshly painted white.

Cell D27-A 204, one of the most secure cells in the prison, had been Marín's residence since the day he was declared guilty in his trial, perhaps even a little later, when he was transferred for being a troublemaker. A solid metal door separated the interior of the cell from the corridor, and a sense of mystery and uncertainty hung in the air. From the hallway, neither of the three men heard a sound. It was as if a beast was contained behind that black door, and it seemed that upon opening it, an almost uncontrollable force would burst forth. It was only moments before a group of guards took position, armed with high-powered weapons, to secure the men awaiting the door's opening. Suddenly, a crazy and out-of-place idea crossed the prison director's mind. The portly man suggested that if there was a chance, they should shoot Marín. He instinctively glanced at General Zapata and explained that Marín had once bitten a guard and almost ripped off his ear.

When the heavy door was opened, an enigmatic white hue on the walls inside contrasted sharply with what the men had seen during their walk through the facility. Finally, when access was granted, the group, accompanied by the prison director, moved toward "El Tío's" cell.

The white walls were carefully adorned with shelves holding books, and a bookshelf that had been crafted with great attention to detail. Zapata observed attentively, first noting works by Engels, Marx, Paul Lafargue, and Sartre. As he moved on, he noticed the names of Bolshevik figures like Bujarin and Herman Gorter, as well as Malatesta. Amid these, somewhat out of place, he found books by Galileo, Plato, and Aristophanes. He then assumed they were facing a well-versed communist. He was about to take one of the books he'd mentally cataloged but stopped himself.

He continued his examination and discovered volumes by Schopenhauer— *The World as Will and Representation*—next to *The Iliad* by Homer. On the other side were works by Walter Benjamin and Foucault, two dictionaries, and two volumes of the *Classical Gredos* collection by Máximo de Tiro. Some worn books caught his attention, particularly a set of *Twenty Thousand Leagues Under the Sea* by Jules Verne, bound in leather. Unable to resist temptation, Zapata took the book, flipped to the chapter "All for Electricity," and noticed it was a bilingual edition with some marginal notes written by the previous reader. He marveled at the presence of books in French and Russian—the Cyrillic alphabet had always fascinated him.

Zapata remained lost in his thoughts, fascinated by the richness of such a library. Karl Radek, Anton Pannekoek, Antonio Gramsci, Trotsky, and Vladimir Lenin—these books showed signs of heavy use. Hans Küng's works on the theology of Abrahamic religions and his global ethics projects were there, alongside Tom Clancy's novels, which Zapata was particularly fond of. He glanced back and carefully examined the books on global ethics. They were marked with highlighters, and some of the advanced theology texts covered topics like "Exitus Reditus" or the fourth-century reforms of the Catholic Church, as well as the reforms from subsequent councils. These were just a small selection from the extensive library. On the other side, there were books on political economy, macro and microeconomics, including works by Thomas Piketty and Thomas Sowell. Also, several political economy books from the 1970s editions by the *Fondo de Cultura Económica* stood out. The sheer number and quality of these volumes amazed the General and reminded him of those years when the military institution had sent him abroad to study.

The General sighed and snapped back to reality. He realized he had been lost in thought for quite a while. Meanwhile, Harlington had remained silent, reflecting on the discipline and order of the man confined in such an exceptionally clean cell. The cell contained handwritten documents with exemplary handwriting, organized in two wooden filing cabinets that Marín had made himself.

The other two men finally noticed Marín sitting in a bamboo rocking chair, clearly crafted by his own hands, suspended from the ceiling of his cell. Besides the chair, there was a table with a bench and a bed. On the table, several African violets were carefully arranged to catch the little sunlight that managed to filter through a crack in the wall, which was likely the only ventilation the room had. The ventilation worked poorly, and the light barely illuminated the interior. On a makeshift table made from cheap wood, there was an Israeli tulip, and attached to the wall, a painting: *The Ninth Wave* by Ivan Aivazovsky. Slowly and carefully, Marín stood up from the rocking chair. He had been reading a heavy photography book by Helmut Newton, which he set aside on one of the nearby shelves before straightening himself.

"Welcome, gentlemen. What brings you to my humble abode?" he said with a smile, showing off perfectly white teeth. "I would offer you coffee if I had any, but I must say the best we get here is some dirty water, as gray as everything else around here, and foul-smelling," he added, grinning. He extended his hand toward Harlington. "Though that last part may not necessarily be true, gentlemen. We manage to get almost anything here, though the privileges are few—privileges, nonetheless."

"Thank you for your courtesy, General... if I may call you that," Harlington hesitated, "I need your help, well, the country needs it."

"Commissioner Harlington, you may call me... whatever you like. If you wish, you could even call me Batman, and I would gladly respond," Marín said, moving toward a small stove connected to what appeared to be a plastic jar filled with water and a few metal bars. He plugged it into an extension coming from the single light bulb in the room. The water began to bubble, and he skillfully ignited a metal burner. He placed a small clay cup filled with water on it. "Two sugars?" he asked as he prepared the coffee.

"I insist, I appreciate your kindness, General Marín. I want—" Harlington began, but then paused, "We want, the gentlemen accompanying me here," he said, pointing to them, "to know what information you have about a kidnapping that took place today around 12:00 PM on the central lanes of the Periférico Sur in Mexico City."

"It was at noon, on the Periférico... let me think for a moment," Marín said, pausing. "I don't know anything more, sir." He continued,

"Generally, those of us locked up here, Doctor, don't know much more than the people out there, walking free on the streets." He took the cup and poured the water into two nearby cups. "Here you go, Colombian coffee from the best harvest."

"Thank you, General," Harlington said, slightly impatient. "But I didn't come here to trade ironies with you."

"I see," Marín replied, serving his own coffee. "I apologize to the rest. I only have two cups. Generally, not many people come to see me, and since my Aunt Pily passed away, I don't receive many visitors... Ah, that's right," he corrected himself with a notably ironic tone, "my Aunt Pily never came to see me either."

Immediately scanning the cell, Marín grabbed a plastic water bottle that seemed to contain potable water. He took out four disposable plastic cups, poured the water, and with a gesture, indicated that they could drink from the cups now resting on the makeshift table.

"... We've come to ask you for a favor, Mr. Marín," said Commissioner Alejandro Harlington, after hesitating slightly.

"We've come to ask you, General, to reveal who kidnapped Senator Fernando Pérez Irigoyen's father. We know you know who it is. If it wasn't you who orchestrated the kidnapping, then it was one of your subordinates. With all due respect, sir, we don't need you to play games with us," General Aragón said firmly.

"Name and rank, sir," Marín replied, without turning to the one who had suggested this idea.

"General, Staff College graduate, Javier Aragón Salas, sir—it's an honor to meet you."

"An honor, General, even under these... unfortunate conditions," Harlington said, taking a sip of the coffee he had prepared. "I must tell you that it wasn't me. Surely, you're mistaken."

"But you may know who did it, sir. I'm going to show you a series of photographs. I want you to be honest with me, General, as brothers-in-arms," Aragón said.

"I will always be honest with a member of the Mexican Army, General Aragón. Now, considering that you might want to help us, what do you offer me? What can I expect from you?" Marín said, finishing his coffee as the words ended.

Marín approached the table, sat down, and carefully removed the new shoots from the African violets, ensuring the plant's shape remained harmonious.

"It's possible to say..." he paused for a brief moment, concentrating on the shoots of another plant. "That here... inside," he said, raising his eyebrows as he gestured to the cell, pointing to the floor where some newspaper clippings were stuck. Harlington and Zapata noticed they were of drug lords executed by the army and navy. "We are all dead. Oblivion is the condition we constantly face, and it's a battle we can't win. As for what little we know, how can I help you?"

"I want you to see these photographs, General," Aragón quickly pulled three photographs from his inner jacket pocket. "Could you tell me if you recognize anything that could give us a lead?"

Marín's expression changed. His face went through several stages—first, surprise flooded his features upon seeing the simple images, then a smile appeared on his lips. He looked at Aragón directly with his deep, black eyes, paused for a moment, and immediately glanced at Alejandro Harlington, offering him an open smile.

"What do you want, Marín? We didn't lock you up here, and I wasn't even in office when you were sentenced," the Commissioner said firmly. "Besides, admit it—you're a criminal who chose his own fate by doing things wrong."

"You don't understand anything, Mr. Harlington," Marín said, as he released the tweezers with which he was expertly trimming the plant, which overflowed with white flowers tinged with purple. He took a deep, audible breath. "The State is The System, meaning it governs every particle of your existence. It decides where I live, with whom you live, how many taxes we pay, and even the reasons behind the taxes we pay or avoid. Both corruption and crime are promoted by a state system that benefits from keeping its citizens in misery."

"Get to the point, General, I don't have time for dissertations on State Theory," Harlington said, his irritation evident. "Do you know something I don't? Speak up!"

"The State dominates through ignorance and filth," Marín said, as Commissioner Harlington screamed and glared at the man trying to explain the world to him. "Alright, the attack took place at least 700 meters away. The shooting range was complicated due to a headwind, and the pedestrian bridge was closed under the pretense of being 'under repair.'"

"Exactly," Aragón said, but he was suspicious of Marín's words. "How do you know that, General? We need names," he shot back.

"To the System, you are just a number—an employee with temporary significance; an honorable or despicable soldier, depending on what the State needs," General Marín said. "In the media, in the collective subconscious, but this is really short in the historical memory of society. On the other hand, the strict symbolic meaning of your activity is that of a minion, reduced to the lowest level," Marín paused and turned his attention back to the plant, resuming his careful tending.

"Don't play games with my patience, damn it, Marín!" Harlington yelled, while Zapata tried to calm him down.

"Look, General Marín, I'm a former military officer. You don't need to know who I am or what I do, but I assure you that once you cooperate with this matter," Zapata declared firmly.

"Mr. Zapata, if I didn't know who you were, I probably would've gone after you and bitten one of your ears off," Marín responded casually. "You work for a mafia that has turned this country into something worse than Rhodesia, and I say that because of the false parliamentary monarchy that they've established in this system of local strongmen that the old politicians have left us with."

There was a brief silence as if Marín were contemplating the coherence of his words, then for a moment, the silence overtook everything.

"What you're saying is a grave mistake," Harlington said, his voice carrying a sense of victory. "I'm no lackey, I'm a free man and a thinker who dignifies himself by listening to ideas." He extended his arms to reinforce the point but couldn't form another word. "What I need are names, not these foolish games."

"There is no System here, you know?" Marín said firmly, raising his voice. He looked flatly at Harlington. "No trust, no hope. All those concepts are left outside. But even for those who don't need the experience in what you call social reintegration — personally, I call it spontaneous incarceration — these concepts exist, and as a result, we are just the entropy of it all, matter that is redundant..." He paused, took a deep breath, and drank from one of the disposable cups. "However, here I have my plants. Look, here's a beautiful violet."

"Damn it, Marín, what do you want... what the hell do you want? Just tell me what you know!" Harlington shouted.

"I truly ask for whatever I want... I want to be the Secretary of National Defense," Marín said, a smile curling on his lips.

"God damn it, stop talking nonsense!" Harlington yelled, losing control.

"Alejandro... Alejandro Mejía, alias 'El Pasa,'" Marín said, breathing heavily. "He's the one responsible, at least the material author."

July 30th, 19:10, Sierra de Santa Catarina, Iztapalapa, Mexico City.

By the time we got up from the table after clearing up a few things, the others pulled out an old deck of cards, worn and frayed with Kings and Jacks. From the back of the table, a deep voice asked, as the cards were dealt, "What made you return to the business, Pasa? You had us neglected for so long. What brings you back now?"

A voice, I said, smiling nervously, because even I didn't know why I had come back. I responded, though my words didn't satisfy anyone present. To be honest, this wasn't my thing. Very few things were. The smile faded from my lips, and my responses faltered into timid words, leaving behind uncomfortable glances.

It wasn't something I was convinced I should discuss, nor did I find it appropriate. However, the inquisitive stares from the other players made me relent, at least partially. I decided to offer them only partial information—nothing that would meet their expectations.

"Five days ago, my phone rang," I said as I dealt the cards from the deck. It was early in the morning. I paused briefly, glancing at the water tank. "It was 3:00 AM. I know because I have an old clock with red glowing numbers right next to my head on the bedside table. I check it every night."

Someone, I decided to recall it privately, on the other side of the line, recognized me, and I recognized them too. I could remember their voice, still soft and velvety, almost perfect, angelically toned. And when I heard it, I knew exactly who it belonged to. In those brief seven minutes we spent on the phone, they sweetly called me by my name, just as they used to many years ago. Their greeting was so comforting, it reminded me of the sensation I had felt with their kiss, long ago. Then they continued with words of affection and warmth. Suddenly, they mentioned they were calling to ask a favor, and went on saying many things that connected me to them— it felt like a communion, as though time hadn't passed at all, as if I had woken up next to them just yesterday. I had no choice but to listen attentively.

The request was for me to meet with an intermediary, and it had to be the next day, in one of the many cafés scattered across the city. I only asked one favor in return, as a sort of payment: I wanted to meet with whoever was hiring me directly, without intermediaries. She hesitated for a moment and told me the only place where we could meet was in a public parking lot. I said I was willing to go wherever she called me. I didn't mention it, but I was desperate to see her, even for just a few minutes.

We both stayed silent, as if trying to shield ourselves from each other, each looking for an excuse. There was something that awakened inside me at that very moment— it felt as if we spontaneously reached an agreement. Deep down, I believe she also wanted to see me. And so, we finally decided to give ourselves the chance to meet. Perhaps it would be like a long-postponed farewell that never took place. But now, it meant something different, though still emotional. We ended up choosing Estadio Azteca as the location for our meeting.

She warned me to go on foot, because they might follow me if I used my car. Who they were, or what their motives were, she never mentioned, but I could imagine no good intentions behind them. As we spoke, my mind began to form ideas, though the excitement of knowing she still thought of me overwhelmed me like a powerful storm, like a volcano erupting. I thought that seeing her again was more important than any danger that might come from going to meet her. I would rather die, thinking of the sweet idea of caressing her face again, gazing into her eyes, than to live a long life in a stale, meaningless existence.

Careful not to mention it, and keeping it to myself, I recalled how she had always had a crucial influence on me. I had admitted long ago that she had control over me from the moment we first met, and it would remain that way until my last breath. We agreed to meet four days after that phone call, the one that had given meaning to my life. When the day arrived, as dawn broke, I prepared myself. It had been a long time since I had enjoyed something like this.

I decided to follow each request, word by word. Maybe it was because I had never been able to forget her and didn't want to upset her in any way. At the threshold of seeing her again, I did it, even with the bitterness in my heart, because my love for her was obsessive and infinite. Though secretly, a trace of hate and contempt lingered in my heart for her. I could feel it. The reason was that when she left me, she destroyed me— at least the best part of me had perished, as in a Mario Benedetti poem. So, for what might have been, I chose to attend the meeting as promised. I did it because the voice I had heard belonged to someone I trusted deeply— perhaps even more than I should have. I decided not to overthink it and focused my thoughts on reconnecting with Yamila.

Although my house, the one I had lived in for a long time, was over three hours away from the famous stadium, I didn't hesitate for a second to cross the city. I wasn't concerned about anything that could stop me from going. When she heard my response on the phone line, agreeing to the conditions she had set for me to see her, I knew she was just as eager to see me. Carefully, I expressed that there were things from our past that hadn't left me fully satisfied. She told me there was much to explain, but we needed to meet in person to do so. I agreed that we should meet, and we both reached the conclusion that our meeting would be strictly professional. Only if the circumstances allowed it, would we take the time to discuss what had happened in our lives since we parted.

At the security house, I avoided the curious and wide-eyed stares of the others. I focused on my cards, ignoring Tinaco and Chucho's expectant gazes, waiting for me to say more about my return to "the business." I knew they wouldn't like it, so as I held the old deck of cards between my fingers, I dealt them and quietly counted the ones I laid out on the table.

In my mind, I replayed every detail of that day, every moment, every sensation. I stared at the pair of kings in my hand, silently changing the rest of my game. Chucho broke the silence.

"Here you go, padrino," he said, blowing on the cards. "I hope you have a good hand."

"Alright, if I lose, you pay for me, okay?" I replied.

"Padrino, did you come back because God spoke to you?" he asked with a small grin.

"Ah, ahijado, you have some wild ideas," I smiled. Something came to mind but quickly slipped away. "I came back to 'the business'... for pure enjoyment."

The room fell silent, disappointed by my words. They seemed insufficient, almost as much as I felt. For a moment, I considered being honest and telling them that the love of my life had called me years after abandoning me, asking me to kidnap someone for her. But I focused on the cards, counting them in my hands, and secretly, furtively, I thought of the unmistakable accent of the Southern girl.

When I saw her, I realized she was just as beautiful as I remembered, though over time, I had forgotten the vividness of her eyes, or her smile. But the moment she saw me approaching, she smiled, and her eyes brought back that sense of life and tenderness I had felt many years before. Maybe she was pretending... I don't know, but for me, the sensation she stirred in me was endlessly sublime.

Seeing her gaze again took me back to the time I lived with her in Playa del Carmen. It was a sweet period. I liked feeling free there. We tried to redesign our way of life, though neither of us had a clue how it should be. From that point on, I found work teaching diving, repairing boats, catamarans, sailboats—anything that broke down on the beach. Our life was far from any idleness, hiding, or weapons. We worked from sunrise to sunset, earned just enough to get by, but life had a higher meaning. Every *peso* and every cent felt worthwhile, liberating. We didn't have to enslave ourselves to anything.

We both tried out many activities. In my opinion, she did better than I did. In Playa del Carmen, she joined a fitness center, a gym looking for people who could offer nutritional advice to members. The truth was, Yamila admitted she'd never exercised before, but she was determined to learn, and her persistence was beyond what anyone could have expected. So, she began teaching cardio, spinning, and other aerobic classes. The pay was low, and it didn't last, but she remembered her childhood ballet lessons, so she applied for a job at a small local academy. She discovered her immense passion for teaching young girls the basic positions of classical ballet. She said she did it more for the love of the art than for the pay.

One day, as her students were leaving class, an agent from the National Migration Service approached her. He asked for her documents, and she replied, in her unmistakable *porteño accent*, that she didn't have any immigration papers. The agent told her that being a foreigner in Mexico was a death sentence, a kind of "direct flight to paradise," and offered her protection in exchange for payment. She refused and ran. The next day, she called the owner of the business where she worked and told her she couldn't come back to teach the girls.

The woman was very sorry but understood the situation. For weeks, Yamila couldn't leave the little house we lived in. Depression drove her mad, and confinement made her furious. A part of her transformed into someone who needed to control everything around her, including me. On my part, I decided to buy a small yacht with my savings, something I had to fix up, and I named it "Yamila." The truth behind the purchase was that it wasn't a luxury—it was a work tool. The idea was to rent out the boat and live off its rental income without breaking the law.

At first, it worked. The boat helped us leave Mexican territorial waters and enter international waters, where we spent time whenever we could. But one day, Yamila told me she wanted to leave. She had seen the National Migration Service agents, and their trucks with the green, white, and red letters of the Ministry of the Interior. She wondered if perhaps "*the Uncle*" had something to do with it, maybe he had some contact in that department, and if she found them, he would take care of them himself.

I agreed with her, partly out of obligation, partly because I realized there was a real possibility she was right. Over time, I understood that the hardest part of leaving behind a life of crime is losing that rush of adrenaline, the constant excitement that runs through your body, and the ease with which you can make a living by committing all kinds of wrongdoings. Something called me to rob a bank or contact someone who could supply me with goods to traffic.

I think from the very beginning, you know it's wrong, but you couldn't care less about what society thinks of you. What you're doing feels like the most exciting thing in life. I had every intention of breaking our pact, getting a weapon, and doing something that would make me feel alive. At some point, you even come to realize that it's the only thing society, God, or whoever you prefer, has left you to truly feel alive.

I remembered how difficult those first months in Cancun had been. The bills were overwhelming, and the small apartment we rented hosted many moments of suffering—a time of scarcity. Yet, in my memories, it will always be the only period of my life when I laughed like never before. I think it was the effect of something I had always been skeptical of: hope. Along with our hope, a love was born, so difficult to describe—something scattered, as exuberant as it was passionate and funny, full of mysteries, yet controlled by the vital need to confirm that we could trust one another.

I learned so much—from sharing blankets with a woman, to feeling worthy of occupying a space in her thoughts. With Yamila, I learned to coexist with her cold hands and feet at night. I learned how to pretend I was asleep, yet stayed awake the whole night, staring at the perfection of her face as she slept next to me. I learned that her warm belly in my hands was unmatched, and her caresses were genuinely priceless. I became accustomed to waking up to her sleepy expression, to feeling secure in her presence. As time passed, we shared a bit more of ourselves.

For a little over a year, our world was reduced to just the two of us. It wasn't entirely idyllic; I wish we could've gone further together, had financial and emotional stability, but to this day, nothing or very little has gone as I wanted. There were moments when I thought we had conquered our destiny, that we had managed to escape that world— the world of death, crime, and the illicit life we had known. But it wasn't like that. No one could've seen everything we still had to live through.

I got up from the poker table and went to the bathroom, where my thoughts returned to certain events, especially the phone call that brought me back into the "business." As I splashed water on my face to clear my mind and ease the growing tension, I felt that I couldn't stay there much longer. My mind drifted back to an earlier time, recalling that early morning when she decided to call after ten years of silence. I remembered how I shrank when I heard her angelic voice. I couldn't help but let a tear—corny and despicable—roll down my cheek. While the words flowed through the phone line to my ears, I realized how strange it was to hear her again after so much time.

Her tenderness never stopped working on me, even after all those years. I had recorded her voice for eternity as a means of attaining an inexplicable sense of well-being, even after all those nights without her, fighting against the cruelty of her absence, battling her disgrace. That night, in the midst of an anxiety attack, I asked, "Are you okay?"—but the question wasn't just out of routine doubt. I expected her to say, "I need you," something that, no matter how much I wanted to deceive myself, never left her lips.

Yamila was smart. She stuck to giving me instructions, and deep down, I know she noticed some trace of desperation in my voice. Without saying it, she asked me to calm down, using that language of complicity that women who know you well can establish. I did it, more out of obligation than desire. During that call, she asked how willing I was to return to the "business." Out of breath, I told her it depended on who asked and how. She said she could imagine, and even resorted to blackmail, though she never made it cheap. She knew it would work on me (and, in fact, it did). I refused to give in at first.

When I was about to hang up, I asked her not to, that I would do whatever she asked, but that I wanted to meet her. Yamila hesitated for just a moment, then, with utmost clarity, told me it was about a kidnapping.

"It's an important man," she said, her voice somewhat subdued. "But I need you to help me. You know I've always trusted you, even with my eyes closed. The client is very generous, but no one, except for me, must know his name. You understand, don't you, honey?"

She explained that the client would give everything, and while she understood I had been away from the business, I was the only person she could trust. She added that she knew I wouldn't refuse, assuring me everything would go smoothly. She told me I would meet the intermediary in a café in downtown Mexico City, where I'd receive the advance and the logistical details. I thought about it for a moment, and then I firmly said:

"No," I told her, "I'll do it, but only if it's you and no one else."

"It'll only take a few minutes," I added, my voice laced with suppressed pleading. "You can explain everything to me better than a third party could. I won't ask any questions—nothing you don't want to answer."

"Darling, you always make me do what you want me to do," she gave in. "Okay, let's do this..."

I'm sure Yamila carefully weighed each of my words and how they might change the situation. After a moment, she agreed. She asked me to come alone, not to drive, to dress discreetly, and that we would meet at the parking lot of the Estadio Azteca at 2:30 p.m. the next day. She emphasized that she trusted my punctuality, then said goodbye with the usual, somewhat cold, "Ciao, a kiss."

I couldn't sleep for the rest of the night. I remembered when we decided to flee Cancún because we suspected Marín was after both of us. His men were obvious, and we preferred to avoid conflict. It was time to return to Mexico. There were reasons to go back. First, years had passed since my crime against *El Gato*, and no one would recognize me. Yamila would be less conspicuous in a place with a larger population, and Marín had no connections in central Mexico—he'd said so himself. Moreover, the democratic change gave us hope for a better life. So, we sold everything we had—what little we owned—including the yacht, the ballet slippers, and the couch where we spent our first nights together. That marked the end of our idyllic life in the Caribbean.

Seven years felt like a long time back then. The death of *El Gato* had faded from memory; no one would remember him—or me. In the neighborhood, life goes on, and forgetting is the same as forgiving; just as forgiveness is the best form of death. One day in April 2001, we arrived at Mexico City's International Airport. There, I found many things had changed, and so had Yamila, as she had been in the capital before Tijuana. We took a taxi from the airport, heading west and then north. With every space we passed, a new story unfolded, which I shared with the woman by my side. She said she had only been in the city for a few days.

I hadn't known she'd been in the capital before; she never talked about her past—where she had been, or anything like that. I never asked. But I do remember one afternoon when I found her kneeling by the bed, holding a large, dark wooden crucifix, praying with tears in her eyes. She looked genuinely moved, and I tried to leave her alone. In all the years I had known her, I had never seen her pray, or even make the sign of the cross. It wasn't something I cared about. My mother had taught me prayers, but after her death—maybe even before—I lost the will to explore whether that heavenly language really served any purpose.

But that day, Yamila prayed fervently, closing her eyes and pressing her hands together. I tried to move quietly, mainly not to interrupt her spiritual experience. As she had this connection, I distanced myself. She raised her face and separated her hands, wiping the tears from her eyes with one hand. She looked at me with her blue eyes and scrutinized me. She asked me to sit beside her. I remember the surroundings—the white bedroom of the house we had found in *Satélite*. The sun poured in through the large window, flooding the room.

She asked me if I believed, pointing to the crucifix on the wall in front of her. I didn't answer her question. Instead, I said that whether I believed or not didn't matter. I would never forbid her from praying or believing in whatever comforted her. I told her that was something I had forgotten somewhere deep in my soul, a place I hadn't visited in a long time and, no matter how hard I tried, couldn't access.

As the sun set over the endless horizon, Yamila told me that on this very same day, many years ago, her father had passed away. She was only five or six years old at the time, and she couldn't remember how it had happened. Not a single memory remained in her mind—no image of her father's face, no scent, no sound of his laughter, not even the sensation of his skin against hers, which had once been so vivid. Yet, she knew that since that day, she had never been happy again.

That sunny afternoon, she shared with me how her mother had remarried a man named Manuel, which led to Yamila running away from her mother's home. She remembered how this despicable man had systematically harassed her, night after night, for a long time, until he had threatened her with a knife. He had also beaten and abused her mother. Over time, both of them became his victims, but eventually, he focused solely on Yamila. By the time she was thirteen, she had decided she couldn't take it anymore and left the roof that had once been her family's.

Yamila had found refuge in the brothels on the outskirts of Buenos Aires, until, as she put it, rolling from bed to bed, she ended up in Bahía Blanca, a city 120 kilometers from her hometown. There, she met one of Wally's associates, presumably also Marín's, who gave her shelter along with eight other girls who worked in the same trade. They provided her with shabby clothes and some basic sustenance, and for several weeks, they took care of her. Even though she was just a girl, they recognized her potential to become a woman of exceptional beauty.

They offered her the chance to come to Mexico, promising her she would make a lot of money. But the real reason she decided to cross the world toward the north wasn't for the money. The truth, deep down, was that she felt terrible about being a prostitute. She feared running into someone who might recognize her, but she didn't know how to do anything else, and survival was a need she couldn't ignore. She accepted everything they offered her, not understanding the magnitude and consequences of that decision at the time. She was sent, along with a group of about twenty-seven girls and teenagers, to Mexico City.

Upon their arrival, they were crammed into a room in a poor neighborhood of the vast city. She didn't know the exact location, as they always left at night and returned at dawn. Besides, everything was so dark and dusty that she had little desire to clarify those details. They were forced to work under deplorable conditions; there wasn't even water in the bathrooms. "We couldn't even wash ourselves. It was the most horrible thing you could imagine," she bitterly recalled.

That situation plunged her into severe depression, especially as she saw many of her fellow travelers suffer, mostly from infections and diseases related to the dreadful hygiene conditions. Each day, she became more concerned about how she would survive the coming days. Nostalgia constantly reminded her of the seven thousand kilometers separating Mexico from Buenos Aires. Sometimes, she tried to console herself by praying, other times she attempted to recall the face of her deceased father, but her efforts were in vain. On many occasions, her mind was overwhelmed by the crushing guilt of having left her mother in the hands of a maniac like Manuel.

It wasn't long before, one fine day, they told us that those who wanted to go to Tijuana should pack their things, the few they had, and be ready. That's how she had ended up with me. She made a journey similar to the one I had taken years before, and I was surprised to learn this after all the time we had spent together. We visited places I felt a connection to, places where I had left a part of myself as I grew up.

I came out of the bathroom, making sure to close the door behind me. I looked at the group playing poker, and Chucho said to me,

- "Godfather, are you going to sit down and play again? You know I bring you luck." he smiled.

- "No, godson." I replied briefly, then glanced at Tinaco and continued, "Partner, are we leaving soon?"

- "The informant called a few minutes ago, Pasa. Nothing's changed, we'll wait a few more hours." Tinaco said, sounding downhearted.

- "If you don't mind, I'll step outside for a cigarette." I said, excusing myself.

- "Go ahead, Señor Pasa, make yourself at home." said María, one of the women present. "Would you like a bench to sit on?"

- "No, Mary, thanks." I replied as I stepped out.

Lost in my thoughts as I smoked, I recalled that five days earlier, I had stepped out from the shadows of the night to meet the woman I knew in the smallest of details.

I decided to wear gray sportswear and go for my usual three-kilometer run, just like every morning since she stopped living with me. With stopwatch in hand and my iPod programmed, I lost myself for forty-five minutes, as I usually did, running along the Bulevar de los Jinetes. On my way back, as I reached the gate of my house, I ran into my neighbor, Gustavo, and greeted him as usual. I picked up the newspaper for the day and had my breakfast—the same cereal I ate every morning along with a cup of tea. I showered, shaved, and left a few tasks on Post-it notes stuck to the fridge door, including a reminder not to forget the betrayals of certain people. I checked the lawn and decided it wasn't necessary to have it mowed again this week.

I wrote a few notes and prepared my outfit for the day—gray jacket, blue shirt, jeans, and comfortable shoes. I considered wearing sneakers, but decided against it in favor of the shoes. From the top shelf of the wardrobe, I took my old gun, the same Glock 17 with a silencer, loaded it with bullets, prepared the three magazines, and checked the condition of the weapon. For a moment, I wondered if perhaps Yamila wanted to kill me. A small firearm with limited ammo and my lack of practice wouldn't offer much defense. Still, I decided to take it, thinking it might serve me somehow and that I would defend myself the best way I knew how, as I had done since the day I was born. At 8:47 AM, my phone rang again, but I didn't answer it.

I left the house at Retorno Marvella #37, in El Dorado, heading toward the parking lot of the Azteca Stadium. During the unbearable drive, with the traffic, noise, and pollution, I made sure no one was following me. I took my time, arriving after a couple of hours at Calzada de Tlalpan. The site where, more than fifty years ago, the iconic cantina "La Hija de Moctezuma" had stood. Now, a shopping center occupied the same space. I decided to park in the supermarket lot and continue my journey on the Metro, making sure to stay alert and avoid being followed.

On the train, which carries millions of people every day, I was careful not to carry any bulky items. The Metro system has magnetic arches to check for firearms, but I managed to bypass the officer asking passengers to cross through the weapon detector. Once inside, I opted to wear dark glasses, aware that some of the many surveillance cameras in the stations were connected to computers that randomly scanned passengers' faces, cross-referencing the data with security agencies. I remained cautious to ensure neither facial recognition nor the weapon I carried would halt my progress. Since my time in Tijuana, I hadn't set foot in a police station, and I didn't plan to now—there was no reason to go back before I started.

My journey would take just a few stations, and then I would board the archaic Tren Ligero of Mexico City, which would take me to the end of my trip. I remained calm, but now, every minute I was stuck in traffic or every time the subway stopped, a memory would come to mind—especially the night she decided that our relationship was over.

Maybe it was the night I rediscovered pain and hopelessness, for I hadn't felt that abandoned since my brother had died. I arrived on time, as usual. From a distance, I could see the stadium, and I scanned it carefully. It seemed like Santa Úrsula hadn't changed at all. By then, it had been many months and years since I'd heard from, seen, or received any news from Yamila. I wondered, deep down, if besides her voice, she had kept those beautiful eyes. During all this time, my bed had remained empty, and only occasionally had my armchair witnessed the end of some fleeting adventure. But those always ended badly.

Moments later, an electric blue BMW, a color unique to the German brand, approached where I was walking. It seemed to be distracted, but I knew better—it was waiting for something. The rear right window rolled down, and a pale hand with short red-painted nails emerged. I recognized it immediately. I approached cautiously. Yamila spoke, asking me if I was alone. I quickly replied that I was, assuring her I'd done things the way she had instructed. I wasn't sure if it had been the best way.

She asked me to get into the car, and I did so willingly, understanding that this was just how things were. She told me I looked thinner and had graying hair as she ran her fingers through it, as if tracing the marks of her absence, perhaps trying to find the teenager she once knew in that dimly lit bar. Then, she excused herself with a smile—her particular smile—and added that she, too, looked older, with graying hair and wrinkles. I pretended not to pay much attention.

She kissed me on the cheek. When she did, I could smell the Oscar de la Renta powder she had worn since we arrived in Mexico. It was a sweet, distinct scent that left a taste in my mouth. I inhaled deeply and could smell the Halloween perfume on her skin. I didn't comment, but she asked me what I had been up to. I didn't answer. Instead, I avoided the question, saying I thought this wasn't an interrogation. She smiled and looked at me intently. I noticed new wrinkles around her eyes and nose, making her appear even more divine. The speed at which she blinked—something I had always found so sweet—captured my attention, and for a moment, our eyes met. We didn't break the gaze for what felt like hours.

"No, no... not at all," she said, slightly uncomfortable. "I just wanted to ask you the questions that good manners dictate, but I don't want to bother you. It seems you haven't changed." She paused without finishing her sentence, then completed it differently: "You're still as stubborn as ever, but as sweet as you were from the very first day."

I looked at her deeply but said nothing, though I was close to saying something like, "the same small-time thug as always," but I held back. That wasn't the case, after all.

"Look..." she said, pulling a cigarette from her purse. She offered me the pack, but I declined. She pulled out a lighter and handed it to me. I lit it while listening carefully.

"Doesn't bother you, right?" she asked in a somewhat mocking tone. I didn't respond, knowing she knew I hadn't smoked since I left "the business."

I told her I wanted to know exactly what was going on, how it would work. I wanted to make a deal and handle things seriously. When I finished speaking, she handed me a black folder. I opened it and found black-and-white photographs. She asked me to look at them carefully, and I did. In each photo, there was a man, likely between 62 and 65 years old. In some, he was playing golf with other men, one of whom I recognized—it was Archbishop Enrique Solís Esquinca of Ecatepec.

I looked at her again and asked who the man was and why they wanted me to kidnap him. She sighed and, with a dissatisfied look, explained briefly that he was the father of a Senator, but she didn't know anything else—just that. I didn't believe her, but I knew she wouldn't tell me if she knew more.

"Yamila, you know I'm here for you," I said with complete sincerity. "I don't kidnap people anymore; I'm a manager at a telecommunications company."

"You were the best, Alejandro..." the Sureña said. "By far, you were the best..."

"Yes, I was... but I'm not the same reckless teenager you met all those years ago," I replied. "We're a little too old to be playing those 'games.'"

"Think about it, honey... for me," she narrowed her eyes. "Don't tell me you're not going to do it now."

There was a brief silence as I looked through the rest of the folder's pages. I didn't press for more details about him or the Senator's son. She interrupted, saying they were offering one and a half million pesos, and my task was to coordinate the kidnapping and removal. The most important part, she emphasized, was that I had to keep him alive—under no circumstances should it get out of control, as mistakes couldn't be allowed. "Your budget is high, as high as you need it to be." The last condition was that the job had to be carried out on July 30th.

As she gave me that information, I thought one and a half million was low, especially for the father of a Senator. A man like him had to be worth more than triple that amount. I even considered suggesting a figure between ten and twelve million—dollars, of course. I thought about negotiating for six or seven million instead. Besides, what did it matter if he stayed alive? Every kidnapper knows the ransom is worth more than the life. Keeping him alive, however, would guarantee a much higher ransom. I looked her straight in the eyes and asked why she wanted me to take care of this. She said she would be honest and gave me two important reasons.

The first was that in the next five days, anyone else would either report it to the authorities, the Senator's family, or handle it themselves. But I would never betray her. The second reason was because she had always admired my guts for doing anything, and she wanted to help me since she felt indebted to me.

There weren't just two reasons, I counted three—but none of them were true. The real reason, I knew, was that she feared things might go wrong. Her next comment confirmed that. "If necessary," she said sweetly, looking me in the eyes, "and things don't go as planned, you need to kill your team, especially your partner. We can't afford to have them talk, give names, or dates. We don't want anything connecting us."

When she finished, I smiled and reassured her, saying not to worry, and that I was dying to know who my team would be.

She immediately interrupted me. In the folder, she said, were the names and photos of seven other men, plus the target. Some were prison intake records, nothing I hadn't seen before, so I shrugged and she simply said, "You choose, take whoever you need. No limits."

A few seconds passed before I told her that the money wasn't enough for me. She knew I had retired, and it would be hard to come back just like that. But before I could finish my sentence, she interrupted, putting her index finger to my lips and then draping her leg over me. She kissed me, the way no one had kissed me in so long, and whispered in my ear, "I don't know if this is your price, but I know it's close."

I couldn't stop myself, nor could I stop her. Her lips and legs made my body tremble, and her hands exploring every part of me made everything culminate in a burst of pleasure. My body couldn't obey reason anymore. Driven purely by instinct, I succumbed to her spell, completely at her mercy. For the next few minutes, I gave in to the fullness of my senses and my deepest desires. The rest of the afternoon was spent together, no reproaches, as good as it had been in the past. When night fell, she dropped me off at my place and said that we were still as good in bed as we had always been. In that moment, I got what I wanted from her, even if it was only half, and she would get what she wanted from me.

I closed the deal. I would do it for the agreed amount. I wanted to do it with just one additional person besides me, "Tinaco." I had heard of him before; it had been a while since I did this kind of thing, but I thought his size and tough look would serve as good recommendations. Over the years, criminals only get bolder. I decided to take a few notes with my cell phone; the next day, I'd meet with everyone involved. I insisted we couldn't trust everything to the folder; we needed to track and verify the information.

Yamila said it wasn't necessary, that it was already late, but she guaranteed all the details in the folder—pointing to the black folder—were accurate. She handed it to me and told me to relax as she adjusted her dress for the umpteenth time.

"You know," she said, "the most important thing is that this is a kidnapping worthy of being televised. I know you can do it. Remember that kidnapping you did with 'El Tío' in Monterrey years ago? When you shot that soldier from a bridge? It would be nice to do something like that. Think about it and do what you do best."

15 Av. Santa Fe #459, 9th floor, Mexico City. 18:04 hrs, July 30th.

In the spacious living room of a ninth-floor apartment, decorated with a white sofa that felt somewhat empty, considering the luxurious building in the most modern area of the country, a man dressed in a black leather jacket toyed with the glasses on the desk in front of him, as the seconds ticked away. He simply spun the pair of glasses with his finger on the wooden surface of the desk.

The man, with a shaved head, breathed steadily, trying to control his tone and manners, which had never been many. He glanced sideways at the two other men with him—one in a military green shirt and the other in a polo shirt with an embroidered logo. While doing this, he mentally reviewed each word and phrase. Almost simultaneously, he picked up the phone. It was one of those older devices with a corded receiver. Despite its outdated appearance, it was connected to a computer. The man in the green shirt worked the communication system, his fingers moving at lightning speed across the keys, while the other man, likely his assistant, watched quietly.

Other indicators from two laptops were pointed out to the man, signaling that everything was ready. Both younger men gave a thumbs-up. The man dialed the number on the rotary phone. After a brief pause, his voice came through, distorted, hollow, and distant—likely due to the computers' interference.

After a few moments, he waited as the phone rang with its usual tones, signaling the incoming call to another part of the city. When it stopped, a weary voice answered on the other end. The man in the black jacket spoke clearly:

"Listen closely, Mariela," he said, focusing on the monitor in front of him, where the instructions were displayed. The screen scrolled slowly, and for a brief moment, something told him that the person on the other end of the line was about to interrupt him. After a nearly imperceptible pause, he continued:

"You don't need to know anything more about me, except the instructions I'm about to give you. These must be followed to the letter if you want your husband to stay safe and return to your arms."

The breath held, still suspended by the distortion from the computers.

In moments like these, having a monitor comes in handy, the criminal thought to himself.

"You can call me 'Z,'" he continued, his tone steady. "I know that all the intelligence agencies, including the Attorney General's Office and CISEN, are monitoring this call. I know every word, every phrase, every breath is being recorded and analyzed, every inflection in my voice. Deep down, I don't really care about any of that, nor do those involved. I also imagine they know that I'm called 'The Uncle,' so let's stop pretending we have any trust in each other and get to business. Let's be professionals, let's be serious."

Meanwhile, Mariela struggled to hold back her tears. Agents from various intelligence agencies signaled to each other, jotting down every word she uttered on a whiteboard with a red marker. Every sob, every unclear sound from her, was recorded and stored. Every word from the man, now identified as "Z," was also captured in the hope of finding something, anything, to continue the trail of the kidnapped man with the white beard.

"Pay close attention, señora," the voice changed tone slightly when addressing her. "Well, actually, you don't have to. The anti-kidnapping division will write everything down on the whiteboard in front of you. Everything I say will be followed, but don't worry, I know how this works. And if you need me to repeat something, I'll gladly do so."

Mariela, overwhelmed, struggled to focus. Her spirits dropped. She wondered if, given how much the kidnapper knew about the system, he might even be in league with one of the agents monitoring her home.

What if one of them had tipped him off about the actions unfolding? For a moment, she felt the strength leave her and wondered if there was any point in continuing, feeling as though her life was slipping away.

"My associates and I want one hundred and seventy million Euros for the life, safety, and well-being of your husband," the voice continued.

There was a brief pause, as though the man were reading from a document, then he added:

"Also, we want you, your husband, your two children, and their spouses to leave the country. You have twelve hours from now to do so."

"The truth is, you and your children make a lovely family," he went on. "We don't want to be forced to eliminate all of you, so I recommend you follow our instructions precisely."

The voice then let out a slight smile, laced with sarcasm, an eerie sound warped by the digital distortion of the phone call, a smile that would haunt Mariela's psyche. Everyone listening could hear the dissonant noise that marked the man's twisted amusement.

For a moment, Mariela thought back to years earlier when such a situation would have been pure fiction, something that had nothing to do with them. But now, with the cold, distant voice issuing its threats, this was her reality.

The voice made a few more warnings, then, with the same mocking tone, addressed the situation at that very moment in the family's house:

"Surely, at this very moment, you're being told to ask me to repeat the instructions. They'll even tell you to repeat them yourself, hoping to trace the origin of this call. Well, I'll indulge them—repeat after me the instructions I've given you."

The voice continued, repeating the instructions rapidly, almost impatiently. Then, he requested that Mariela repeat them back to him. Once she had finished, he paused before issuing one final warning:

"Very well, Mariela... is that what they call you, right? Now they'll tell you that the call is coming from Tlaxcala Street, in a neighborhood near the city center. God only knows how many patrols are on their way to that location."

The Federal Police technicians exchanged confused glances, as the location data confirmed what the criminal had just said.

The voice paused for a long moment, and one of the technicians signaled that the call was still "connected."

"You know the surprise they'll get when the officers who arrive at the address find a pair of elderly people living in the apartment from which this call supposedly came," the man mocked. "Anyway, they'll never stop being gullible, parasitic idiots—police, do you hear me?"

He shouted, then suggested connecting Raúl with Mariela, saying it would make sure they treated him like royalty, even better than Alicia, his lover had. But he quickly contradicted himself, realizing it wasn't the right moment.

"I have to hang up now, Mariela. This isn't the only business I need to sort out. You understand, don't you? Life's very expensive these days, and especially short."

When the call ended, a void filled the room. Everyone was desperate for some sign that Raúl was still alive, but nothing could provide that assurance.

Julián Alaminos didn't say anything, but deep down, he felt a sense of self-repulsion. Nevertheless, he picked up the phone and stepped into the garden of the house where he had been for several hours. He dialed the number, but just before he could finish, he stopped. He thought that perhaps his friend was dead, maybe lying in some ravine or in one of the many rivers in the city, which served as the final resting place for hundreds of unclaimed bodies. What an unfair fate, he thought silently, while smoking the last cigar his friend Raúl had given him. But the worst mistake anyone could make was not to take advantage of Alicia.

Perhaps she could be involved, and if that were the case, he would need a lawyer—someone good. One of the interns at the firm could handle the case with advice from Mouriño, one of the best in the office. In the end, his friend would understand. It would be like taking care of her in his memory. After all, the road to hell is paved with good intentions. They say the best business is to be both the cure and the cause of a problem.

Finishing his cigar, Alaminos decided to call Alicia Bahena. He would inform her of what little he knew about Raúl. He considered telling her that the most likely scenario was that Raúl was dead, and she would have to accept it and find comfort in knowing that was his fate. But he thought too much about it while watching the clock tick, imagining the agonizing minutes Raúl was enduring, if he was still alive.

He held back with Alicia; he didn't want to speak without facts or proof. He wasn't going to tell her that the kidnappers might have already ended the life of the only man who had ever taken care of her. Instead, he would say they had contacted the family, and that Mariela had spoken with them. He would tell her that Mariela had done well, and they now knew with some certainty that the kidnappers demanded a large sum of money, and that the situation was delicate but under control.

He followed through with this plan while walking to the corner of the garden where the perimeter wall met. He pulled his phone from his jacket pocket, found Alicia's number, dialed it, and waited. He didn't say much, but Julián assumed she understood the meaning behind his words, even though she didn't fully grasp them.

The man with the shaved head made a call to the safe house, where the staff informed him that everything was calm. "Z" instructed them to keep the line open and put Raúl on the phone so he could speak with his family. After a few moments, "Z" took the phone again and dialed a number on the fixed line. His assistants observed the computer screens, signaling that the call was in progress. Moments later, the phone rang three times, and Mariela answered. Tension filled the room as over half a dozen agents tried to trace the call's origin.

It soon became clear that this was a three-way call interface. The criminal warned that there was a surprise. Now, a voice, noticeably tired and weak, came through, distorted but recognizable as Raúl's. Those listening in Mariela's house couldn't be sure, but the voice sounded worn out. Raúl confirmed he was okay, mentioned that they had given him his insulin and fed him, reassuring his family about his safety. This news brought some relief, as it addressed one of their main concerns. A slight sense of calm spread through the room, at least now there was proof that the victim was still alive.

"Z" told Raúl's wife that the Federal agents would give another location for the call's origin but warned her not to rely too heavily on it. He advised her that the best course of action was to follow the instructions carefully, and that way, she could recover what had been lost in the previous hours. The agents monitoring the data were surprised to see the call's origin was now showing as coming from a neighborhood in the northern part of the city. This was technically impossible, though—the distance was over two hundred kilometers from the previous location. It was a landline, which was already unusual, and it would have been impossible to cover that distance in just four minutes, even by helicopter.

The equipment they were using in the command center was the most advanced and well-calibrated in the country, so how could this be happening? Everything the voice had described matched up perfectly. The police had conducted a massive operation in the area of Pintores Street in Loma Bonita, Tlaxcala, raiding the department they believed the call came from, but they only found two elderly people who had no idea why fifty officers had shown up at their home. The security cameras confirmed no one had entered or exited the apartment. The media was alerted, but once it was proven unlikely that this had been the call's origin, the authorities' incompetence was once again exposed.

Another large group of officers headed to the Electra neighborhood in the State of Mexico, where the second call was supposedly placed. The result was the same: an abandoned building with no signs of a kidnapping. The police now suspected two different people in far-off locations, but they still needed to figure out which side of the city the kidnapped man was being held.

The family was at a loss, the feeling of despair thick in the air. For the first time, they understood that it was very likely they would never see the head of the Pérez Irigoyen family again. Mariela, in a panic, spoke with Fernando, leading him discreetly into the kitchen. She spoke in a low but desperate voice, telling him that he had to comply with the kidnappers' demands because his father's life was truly at risk. She made it clear that the police were useless, with no leads or signs to give them hope. She also emphasized that it made no sense to trust them with something they were clearly unqualified to handle, as the kidnappers were toying with them and mocking their position.

"We can go to the McAllen house. We'll be there for a while. Nothing is more important than being together again. Please, son. Do whatever is in your power..." Mariela told Fernando.

The Senator sighed, reflecting on his mother's pleading words. After a moment of contemplation, he finally agreed to do as she asked: they would accept the captors' demands, with no hope of stopping them.

Fernando asked his mother what she wanted them to do. She took comfort in suggesting they pay the ransom and leave the country. The Senator walked along the corridor leading to the kitchen, preparing to make a phone call, when a deep voice interrupted him. Julian Alaminos pointed out that the sum the kidnappers demanded was astronomical and not easily attainable. As a lawyer, he recommended that he personally negotiate the ransom, aiming to lower the amount. He reminded them of his experience with such matters, having dealt with similar situations in Colombia. There were other options, he said, all of which were preferable to the surrender that the family was contemplating.

He also suggested that Fernando renounce his political career—his presidential aspirations—something that would come at an incalculable cost. A tinge of bitterness crept into his voice as he made the remark. Fernando looked at his godfather with tense composure, diplomatically thanking him for his advice, but firmly insisting that his family's well-being had no price.

Money was another matter. It was a vast sum, but the family gathered together to assess what they could come up with. Fernando concluded it was time to cash in the favors his Senate office had earned him. He made some calls, personally handling the financial discussions, and instructed Rosario Schafter to reach out to every friend and politician in her contact list for help.

Deep down, Fernando knew he would blackmail President Trevilla. How? That was easy. He had several excuses to justify his actions. The first was the nation's overwhelming insecurity—anyone in their right mind would feel a deep knot in their throat, realizing that anyone could be a victim of the tragic and traumatic event his family was now enduring. All it would take were a few television interviews, two magazine covers, a front-page story, and a couple of columns to highlight the violence and fear that had overtaken the country.

Being the most popular opposition senator, with a clear and consistent political track record, would be useful for transmitting these emotions to the nation. Everyone knew this, including the President, Fernando, and many others. Another lever was his friend, the Head of Government of Mexico City, who would certainly help and provide the necessary funds.

But there was one detail that almost everyone overlooked. The kidnappers had made it crystal clear: "The entire family of Engineer Raúl must leave the country, including his children and their spouses." Was Lucía, Fernando's ex-wife, included in this deal? What about her?

It seemed absurd to ask the kidnappers what to do in the case of a divorce.

Lucía had rebuilt her life. Just a few weeks ago, she had been appointed the director of a prestigious fashion magazine—her dream since she was twenty. Now, she had a large office, two assistants, and was invited to every fashion event in the city and even the country. She had attended Milan Fashion Week and, at last, the designers she had admired since adolescence granted interviews with her publication, treated her as an equal, and invited her to dinners without hesitation. She also had a relationship with a Brazilian model, making her the envy of the social elite.

It was clear that Lucía would think Fernando's request to "accompany him and his family on their flight from the country" was nothing but a jealous outburst. But, surprisingly, the doubt didn't come from Fernando—it had been planted in his sister's mind. Upon hearing the kidnappers' words, she had sharpened her focus and quickly contacted her husband, Adbul Manzur, warning him not to return to the country under any circumstances.

Meanwhile, the Senator stared at his mobile phone, momentarily frozen. It was clear he was weighing his words—how to say them and in what tone. He dialed the President's private line, a number he had kept for some time. When Mariana, Fidel Trevilla's personal secretary, answered, it took just a brief introduction for her to assure him that she would connect him to the President. After a moment, a deep voice responded with the seriousness and precision the situation demanded.

Fernando thanked him for the courtesy, quickly informing him of the demands made by the kidnappers. He explained that, as was evident, he did not even come close to having the amount of money the criminals were asking for, that the police had no accurate information about his father's whereabouts, and they had been unable to identify the culprits. He also mentioned that time, according to the experts and his family, was running out. He concluded by acknowledging the deep despair and hopelessness he was feeling at that moment.

From the very first moment, the President seemed to understand. The conversation shifted to a more human than political level, something that any president could afford to do very rarely. Fidel Trevilla saw a clear path to resolving his problems. When the Senator asked for financial assistance, the President only needed to respond that the presidential office was fully committed to helping him in this difficult situation. He also assured him that, as President, he would always be ready to support a patriot. Fernando expressed his gratitude once more, realizing that money would no longer be a concern.

Fidel knew that if he managed to get rid of Fernando, he and his party would have a near-certain victory. At the very least, they would feel less pressure and could act more coherently in the upcoming elections. Moreover, if they managed to bring the Senator's father back alive, it would be less of a problem. It would show that they had upheld the security and integrity of the citizens. Fidel also considered that his team might be able to trace the money, and with all the back-and-forth, it was likely to be distributed among several members of the cabinet.

Fidel Trevilla asked for some details, and immediately directed the matter to "someone who would resolve it," a person who would be in charge of handling the situation with the Senator's personal secretary.

Before ending the call, they reached an agreement: the money would be delivered to the residence in Las Arboledas. As agreed, two hours later, a security van arrived, carrying 172 million Euros. All the bills were marked, except for two million, which were in marked bags and counted as additional funds.

16. Almoloya de Juárez, State of Mexico. 18:15 hrs, July 30th.

Alejandro Harlington had been struck by a series of fleeting ideas, like flashes of light illuminating his mind. Now, a man in military attire with a shaved head had joined the group. General Aragón, one of the men he trusted most, handed him a detailed report about the calls made by the federal police. The police had concluded that the so-called "Tío" was imprisoned in the high-security prison of La Palma, in Almoloya de Juárez. In other words, Marín was not the mastermind behind these events. Moments before, there had been a brief exchange of words.

"In an email intercepted by intelligence," said General Aragón, "you are mentioned in connection with the kidnappers of Senator Pérez Irigoyen's father. That's why we're here. You know where the man from your cell is, but instead of condemning you for your crimes, we propose offering you your freedom, provided you tell us the whereabouts of Mr. Raúl Pérez." He turned to Marín as he spoke.

"How can you be sure you're speaking to the person you're looking for?" Marín replied, picking up a gray-covered book. "I mean, I'm not Socrates, Muhammad, or Jesus Christ. Tell me, General, what exactly did the message say?"

"It's you," Harlington said. "They called you 'Tío,' Guillermo... The message said they had spoken with 'the Tío' from Monterrey. In our database, there were many criminals who went by the name 'Tío,' but none from Monterrey who are still alive."

"Right there, that's your problem, Commissioner," said General Marín, his voice calm, like that of a teacher explaining to students. "The nickname 'Tío' isn't just an alias—it's a rank in the criminal hierarchy. It's a title you only earn by displacing the previous 'Tío.' Let me explain, there are many who once were my friends who now believe I'm dead.

But let's not get into ontological debates. The 'Tío' you're looking for is someone I know well. He's in this photo, Doctor Harlington—the dark-skinned man you're searching for, along with another fat guy. This photo was taken about fifty-eight hours ago, or something like that, according to the markings on the side."

"Who is this man?" Harlington demanded, his desperation growing. "I demand you tell me everything you know about this man, now!"

"The Wally..." Marín paused for a long moment. "But this is where the real negotiation begins. I want my freedom, and a dignified way to survive once this—this big favor—is over," he said impulsively.

"Yes, yes, that's a given. Now tell me how we can find this Wally, or whatever his name is," Harlington said, his voice tinged with desperation. "I'll give you back your military rank and complete freedom. What else do you want, damn it?"

"...So, the idea of becoming the Secretary of Defense, I should just forget about it, right?" A macabre smile spread across the prisoner's face. "We need to get out of here. Alejandro Mejía was a troubled teenager when he arrived in Monterrey, where I trained him under a strict military regime. He became a ruthless killer from a very young age. As he told me, he lost his brother and his mother; he rarely spoke of his father. For years, he served me, and I protected him. I sent him to Tijuana after some problems in Monterrey. There, he met a woman named Yamila. If my memory serves me correctly, she was a prostitute who cast a spell on him. The last time I heard of them was in 1999, when they were in Cancún and then Playa del Carmen. But if you get me out of here right now, I'll finish telling you what I know on the way."

17. Club de Golf "La Hacienda", Atizapán de Zaragoza, State of Mexico. 18:38 hrs, July 30th.

Lucía, the ex-wife of the Senator, arrived at the house of her former in-laws. There, she met with her ex-sister-in-law, and the two of them talked for a long time. They had been close friends since high school, even though Lucía was younger than Valeria. They shared a genuine sisterly love, and when their conversation ended, they embraced to reaffirm their bond. For the first time during these tragic events, Valeria cried—cried like never before, without restraint, without holding back.

Fernando sat in the living room, watching them from a distance, like someone observing a spectacle from another race to which he didn't belong. For a few moments, he felt offended. It was unacceptable that his sister was crying on the shoulder of a stranger. Wasn't he there for that purpose? He didn't say anything, deciding to stop thinking about it, but a slight bitterness crept up on him amid his confusion.

Lucía greeted everyone naturally, except for Fernando, to whom she simply said, "Hey, what have you been up to?" He responded curtly, "Good, not much." This irritated him further, as deep down, it hurt him. She clearly knew that things weren't going well for him, but she had no other words for him. She understood the gravity of his father being kidnapped and the lack of news about his condition. She also understood the stress of his political career, which was always hanging by a thread. But there she was, offering no comforting words, not a single show of affection or care. He deserved none of that, and it was making him sick. The only thing that kept him grounded in his fragile sanity was that Lucía hadn't brought her idiot new boyfriend along.

Few things could complicate the situation more than the thought that, by the next legislative session, he might no longer be a Senator. As unlikely as it seemed, he would have to figure out how to spend his time. For him, his entire life had been about working in politics. He had been doing it since he was sixteen. He had chosen not to study engineering, as the last three generations of his family had, in order to fulfill his dream: to serve his country in its highest office.

Now, looking at it all, it was incredible how one dream could give his life such meaning. By breaking away from the model his family had followed, he had to forge his own path. Even though he always had the valuable advice of his family, especially his father, there had never been concrete answers about how to behave in a world where everything is difficult—especially when it comes to surviving and thriving. From school on, he participated in every oratory competition he could, and in college, he won every election he entered. By then, he was already known as a brilliant politician.

He knew from a young age how to combine two key aspects: his image with a fluid and approachable character. By the age of twenty-six, he had been elected as a Local Congressman in the district where he had grown up. By twenty-nine, he was appointed Deputy Secretary of Programming and Budget at the Ministry of Finance. By thirty-three, he had been considered a potential candidate for Governor of the State of Mexico from the right-wing faction, though he was never publicly announced to avoid damaging his reputation. At least, that was the rumor among those most familiar with the political landscape.

In the end, the candidate was the great-nephew of one of the party's founders. He lost, and by that time, many speculated that there had been an important negotiation to make the presidential campaign fully democratic. However, Pérez Irigoyen was appointed as Senator for the State of Mexico through proportional representation, a position he had reached at just thirty-five years old.

A few months ago, a rumor had spread suggesting that the Mexican right already had a solid, capable candidate—and it wasn't Pérez Irigoyen. As the weeks passed, and he tried to ignore the whispers about this news, the team of analysts working for him confirmed that it wasn't just speculation. Now, he faced the possibility of losing everything—everything that had defined him and made him feel like someone worthwhile. At times, all he felt about himself was fear and disappointment.

For a moment, all these thoughts overwhelmed him, and he suddenly felt slumped on the couch in the second-floor living room of his parents' house. From the pocket of his suit, he pulled out a small white and blue pillbox—it was Altruline. He swallowed a pill whole, without water. He had been taking them for a while now, ever since the separation and the subsequent divorce. He felt so depressed, so desolate, and, most of all, so alone. Now, as he looked at the pillbox, he realized that it was a new one—he had just started a new pack that morning.

He stared at the pills as if hoping they would offer him some sort of answer. He felt both suspicion and aversion toward the medication, perhaps the same disgust he felt toward himself. He went over to the library desk, pulled out a blank sheet of paper from the drawer, took a pen, and tried to write—at least, he believed he was writing. It was a letter addressed to the public, but the words wouldn't flow. Despite his efforts, his trembling hand and lack of clarity in his thoughts prevented him from making much progress.

In it, he tried to explain the reasons for his withdrawal from the political scene. He lamented how the country's democratic life was crumbling due to insecurity. He would argue that serving his country had been the greatest honor of his life. He would implore politicians from all factions to come together and transform what was necessary to face the crisis of violence and fear that was suffocating regions of the country—regions that were pushing the state to the brink of ungovernability due to a lack of peace and social justice.

He tried several times, and after much effort, one of the letters became somewhat legible. In it, he expressed the immense pain he felt at having to prematurely end a career he said would never truly end.

When he finished, he read it. The pain was almost indescribable. His chest tightened, making it hard to breathe, and the only relief came when a few tears rolled down his cheeks. It felt so unjust—he had dedicated his entire life to this work, only to be forced to leave it all behind.

He poured himself a shot of tequila and drank it in one gulp. He felt it burn down his throat, and for a brief moment, the strong flavor of the drink distracted him from his thoughts. But the tears didn't stop as he sat there, continuing to drink while listening to Liszt. He let each tear flow freely down his cheeks. After a while, he noticed two large, bright eyes watching him from the other side of the room. Fernando met them with his red, tear-filled eyes.

"I understand it's hard," said Lucía, the owner of the large, dark eyes, as she looked at him from across the room. "But you don't have to hide, Fer. It's only natural that you're worried about your dad; we all are, believe me," she added as she took a seat next to him. "But he's strong, just like you."

Fernando looked at her, realizing how much he enjoyed looking at her. He sighed and told her that he wished he had been as strong as his father. Lucía embraced him, like a mother comforting a child who had just lost a soccer match, or one who had dropped their ice cream before finishing it. Fernando thought that, perhaps, in another time, he would have been offended by Lucía's gesture. But today, he preferred this hug of pity and compassion over being alone with no sign of affection.

He had so many things he wanted to say—things that surely would have made sense—but the words never made it past his throat. For a few minutes, they stayed embraced, as if time had stopped and hours had no meaning. It felt as if no day had passed since their last night together.

One of the officers from the Attorney General's office came upstairs looking for the Senator. He informed him that the money had arrived—it was time to proceed. The cynical "Z" had provided them with a phone number to call once they had the money he demanded. It was time to take the next step.

Fernando would be the one to make the call and receive instructions from "Z." After the counting of the money in the living room of the Senator's parents' house, thirty large suitcases filled with thousands of euros in different denominations were placed around the room. They were systematically counted using special equipment, opened one by one, and sealed again to ensure that no money was missing. The money had to be placed in the most visible spot possible, Fernando instructed those handling the suitcases.

In just minutes, with the help of twenty bill-counting machines, the task was completed and it was confirmed that everything was in order.

Fernando took the phone and dialed "Z." The conversation was tense and heated, but the Senator, who was adept at handling complicated negotiations, managed to get through it without incident. This time, however, he would limit himself to following orders—a concept that was almost foreign to him.

When "Z" answered the phone, he simply asked: "Do you have the money?"

"Yes," the Senator replied, his voice firm. "Now I ask you to release my father," he insisted.

"Senator, what a pleasant surprise!" came the distorted voice on the other end.

"You have my word that my immediate family will leave the country," Fernando paused, his voice heavy with regret. "Including myself. We won't return for a long time."

"Your wife and you..." the voice said with malicious intent, in a gravelly tone.

"My ex-wife," Fernando corrected, his voice steady. "She doesn't have to accept the rules of this absurd game of yours. She is no longer part of this family," he added firmly.

"Not part of your family?" The voice chuckled darkly. "Tell me, what would she be doing right now in your house, if, as you claim, she is no longer part of your family?" Another laugh escaped the speaker. "I know everything, Senator. I know who's there, who comes and goes, why and how. Now listen carefully." The voice on the line sounded especially determined. "Follow my instructions, and as I'm sure I'm on speakerphone, she already knows she must leave with you."

"First," the voice continued, "the money that the security company brought must be placed in the Senator's Mercedes, no tricks. The suitcases will barely fit between the trunk, back seat, and passenger seat, but they will fit. They will be taken to the Mexico City International Airport, to a private hangar named Aerolíneas Lovely Express. Once there, the Senator will find a note directing him to where he will pick up his father. Your family and you will board the flight that suits you best, but all of this must be done before midnight."

Fernando repeated each of the instructions. In the end, he hung up, feeling frustrated that he couldn't oppose his father's captor's will. The preparations only took a few minutes. It was decided that they would fly to McAllen, and their valuables would be shipped in an international move arranged by the house staff.

Fernando looked at Lucía, a beautiful woman with large black eyes, and asked if she would go with them. She gazed at him sweetly and said she would follow them to the ends of the Earth, as long as it was for something as important as saving a life. Lucía would go to her house to collect her documents and explain to her work that she was leaving the country. Her boyfriend would understand.

They left in different vehicles. Fernando drove the Mercedes Benz, which was almost full with the money, leaving little space for him, which meant he was escorted by two patrol cars to the airport. In his mother's van were Mariela, Vale, and Lucía. His ex-wife would head back to her single-life home in a red car, and they would meet at the airport at 10:00 PM. Along the way, Fernando's mother and sister lamented the misfortune of the dark day that had unfolded.

July 30th, 19:48 hours. Santa Fe Avenue #459, 9th floor, Mexico City.

When the agents arrived and began their search of the property listed under Carmelo Pérez's fiscal identity documents in Mexico City, they only found piles of telecommunications equipment, similar to what police departments used—cell phones and laptops, most of which were broken, clearly smashed with a hammer or similar objects. Some were magnetized to erase information from their hard drives. They also found shredded papers and garbage bins filled with destroyed documents, possibly anticipating such an outcome.

In one of the bedrooms, a small printed agenda barely peeked out from the trash can. It caught the attention of one of the agents, who, using latex gloves, carefully flipped through it. The agenda contained only a few names, all neatly written, with a slow and deliberate handwriting, all in black ink. The agent was impressed by the precision with which it had been written. The names were arranged alphabetically, and there were no signs that anything was out of place. However, one particular entry stood out—a phone number written in red ink, in a different handwriting and out of alphabetical order. It was the name of a woman, an unusual one: Yamila Marconi.

By the time Commissioner Alejandro Harlington arrived, the team had already focused on the agent's intuition, which had led them to the crucial piece of information. When Harlington saw it, he didn't react much, but General Aragón took note. For Guillermo Marín, it was different. The name immediately triggered a memory, sending his mind racing. He remembered a thin young woman who had come from Argentina to work for one of his businesses. He'd seen her once or twice—once at "Jake Mate," maybe at a party, but it wasn't important. What mattered was that he remembered her, and it would be easy to find her. A phone call would suffice.

Marín recalled the technology left behind, reminding him of an occasion when he had bought something similar to deceive someone. Harlington seemed indifferent, but Aragón gave Marín some credit. The same phone line that Marín was sure would receive calls frequently—it wasn't a coincidence. Moreover, with a voice synthesizer, they could mask their voices, turning them into the "Uncle."

Marín asked for permission to handle the job, which Harlington granted. They watched as Marín, with the help of a technician, set up the phone line. Within minutes, after a lot of effort, the equipment worked. Meanwhile, other police technicians scrambled to recover more data from the computers, trying to piece together papers with the hope of finding any connection. Once the phone was ready, the speakerphone rang.

A female voice answered:

"Hello?" she asked, waiting in suspense. "Uncle? What do you want now?" she added, clearly annoyed.

"Where are you?" Marín asked.

"On my way to the airport. The mess is all settled," she paused and hesitated. "You know already, right? The boss just confirmed it. It seems we'll leave sooner than planned. And well... what about you?"

July 30th, Sierra de Santa Catarina, Iztapalapa, Mexico City. 19:47 hrs.

At some point, everyone thinks about death, and occasionally, we also think about life. Raúl Pérez thought his death had arrived—that any moment could bring the end, in a way he least expected. It would be like an unfinished summary, just as everything he had done in life had always been, but how would it happen? They would lift him, allowing him to see the faces of his killers. They would make him kneel and shoot him in the back. Would there be a place to go afterward? Would anyone remember who he had been? There were more questions than answers, and in his mind, everything was spinning. Nonsensical images filled his thoughts. He thought about time and how fleeting it was—how strange it is to think of it without ever truly enjoying it. He wanted to scream, to beg for release from this terrible suffering of awareness.

He thought briefly about his family. It pained him deeply to end like this. What would his children think of him? Would they suffer? It felt unfair to give them another reason to suffer because of him. He also thought of Alicia Bahena and all the nights she had given him... well, no, it was a mistake to think she had given them to him entirely, but at this point, it didn't matter how freely the sensations, the kisses, or the caresses had been given. Had she been the one who had betrayed him? She knew his car, his schedule, and even knew about his children. Could she have turned him in? Seconds, minutes, and hours passed aimlessly. He was suspended, motionless, with his hands bound. This was the worst state they could have kept him in.

All these thoughts rushed through his mind, making him think that nothing had been more important than those forbidden nights in that Polanco apartment—nights he had kept secret for many years. But the thoughts were cyclical, and he kept going back to Alicia. There was no one else in the world who had any reason to capture him. In the past, he had received many threats, none of which had come true, but now he was just an old, decrepit man, and no one cared to threaten him anymore.

He tried to remember his thoughts from that rainy morning but couldn't. He didn't know what the last words he had said to Sergio were. You think everything will go on the same forever, that you'll have time to apologize to your loved ones, but life shows you that it's not like that. None of his morning thoughts came back to him. Everything was spinning. He had been awake for hours, but motionless. Perhaps more than ten hours had passed, but it was impossible to know. He counted his breath to track time, but he couldn't be sure. He had never been in such a state before.

Suddenly, a hand grabbed his shoulder, pulling him from his thoughts and introspection. For a moment, he thought the hand would drag him outside and shoot him. That would be the end, surely. The man holding the hand would make sure not to stain himself with his blood—assassins don't like getting blood on them, he thought.

Who would remember him? What an idiot! He lamented over the least important things, he concluded to himself, as he was dragged through the narrow corridor toward the outside by his captor's strong arm. Then, he tried to remember the faces of his children. He did it consciously, with all his effort, knowing he would never see them again. First, his daughter's beautiful eyes—dark, deep, expressive, and lively, or at least they had been before. It had been a long time since he had looked her in the eyes. He couldn't; it had been since she confronted him about his relationship with Alicia, the time she had responded, unaware that she was his lover. His daughter had confronted him, accusing him of always preferring his "affairs" over being with them. It had been two and a half years since then, and since that moment, their gazes always avoided each other.

His daughter was a strong woman; she had been so ever since she was just a little girl, when he left and she suffered so much that she promised herself never to suffer for anyone again. She didn't like her marriage to the Lebanese man, but she had no moral grounds to tell him so, having kept it a secret for a long time.

As for Fernando, he only wished his son knew how much pride he had always taken in him, even though he had never said it aloud. Beyond his political and legal achievements, beyond being a senator, undersecretary of revenues, he had always been his son—the only child he had, one who, in his mind, surpassed anything he could have imagined. Fernando had known about his affairs and romantic slip-ups since he was six years old. He had told him so during a drink they shared together in the living room. He wasn't angry when he said it; on the contrary, he explained that he now understood why Raúl had sought these romances: to feel good about himself. Raúl stared deeply at his son, unsure of how to respond. Fernando held his gaze and said he was probably the only one in the family who could understand him.

"Have you told your mother?" Raúl asked his son. "I don't want us to have any more arguments over this."

"No, obviously, I won't," Fernando answered. "But tell me, what made you marry my mother?" He hesitated, genuinely curious.

"I don't know, we were young..." Raúl replied honestly.

Had there ever been a moment when he could have answered that question? No... but still, he tried to remember, even as his body was dragged across the floor like a lifeless sack. He decided to block out all physical sensations, imagining himself as a sack of potatoes, being pulled by the brute force of an unknown hand. He clung to his memories, squeezing his eyes shut so tightly that a tear rolled down his cheek and into his mouth, its salty taste revealing it to be a long-held tear.

He thought about how much he would have liked to tell his daughter how much he loved her, to see her beautiful eyes again, even for a fleeting moment. That would have been enough to ease the pain that now overwhelmed him. The hand loosened for a brief moment, and he collapsed, drained of all strength, continuing to lie motionless. Then he clung even more tightly to his memory, trying to recall her face. He sighed as he imagined her thick eyebrows, her straight nose, full lips, and sharp jawline that formed a beautiful composition. He thought again about her eyebrows, realizing they gave her face so much personality and character.

He returned to the image of Valeria's nose. All his thoughts focused on that part of his daughter's face. From the front, it was distinctly turned up, while from the side, it was slightly aquiline. Her mouth, with its perfectly shaped lips, formed a gesture—a unique, indescribable one—that made her who she was. For a moment, he thought about his daughter's mouth, imagining a warm smile, but the memory of her entire face also faded, and for a brief moment, a deep and real fear gripped him—the fear that he might never see her again. His fears vanished like clouds on a windy day, and the memory disappeared as well. He was ready to face death, to embrace it and let it consume him.

He thought of Fernando, but preferred to remember him as a child. He felt immense satisfaction remembering how much Fernando resembled him. He also wished he could have told him not to give up on his dreams, that yes, he believed his destiny was with Lucía. He should go for her, fight for her, whether or not he won the presidency. In any case, Fernando would always be his favorite person in life. He regretted the hurt he had caused Fernando as a child, but it had never been directly because of him. It had been life and its incomprehensible trials that made it so. His absence and abandonment had never been his fault, nor his sister's, nor his mother's. It had been entirely his fault, and he was ready to be judged for it.

As what he believed were his final moments drew near, he dedicated them to his wife—the kind woman who had forgiven all his infidelities, all the affairs that had ended in just that—simple affairs that consumed his mind for weeks or months, but always ended up being a mistake. She had never once reproached him, even though Mariela knew about the other women. She had always treated him with kindness and respect. He would have loved to say a few words to her, to tell her how much she had meant in his life, how he recognized that as a wife, she had devoted herself to him, and as a mother, she had been exemplary in every way. He wished he could tell her that he had loved her, in his own way, as everyone loves in their own way, according to their own understanding of love.

He also realized that he couldn't remember her as she was now, but as he had first known her, many years ago, when she was a young girl from Guanajuato who had come to the big city. He concluded that he had been dead inside for many years, though he hadn't realized it at the time.

Whatever was left in the next moments would only complete a process he had entered, who knows when.

Raúl was somewhat surprised when he felt himself being thrown into a vehicle again, perhaps the same one he had been transported in earlier, though he couldn't be sure. The person who had dragged him along also boarded the vehicle. He knew it was a heavy-set man because he could feel the van shift, no longer level with the ground. He didn't speak, not even trying to, but he suspected that for his captors, it would be easier to kill him in some desolate place far from where he had been held earlier. Perhaps they had realized he was related to someone highly public, and panic set in. They thought it would be better to dump him far away, rather than keep him at their house or in a safe house. He would be left on some road, and if luck was on his side, he might be abandoned there—maybe even freed—or he could end up as food for starving dogs. He didn't care. If that happened, perhaps it would allow his son to escape the consequences of his mistakes. Maybe his death would finally earn his wife and daughter's genuine forgiveness.

He sank deeper into the melancholy space he had created for himself. He imagined he was heading to the place where his mind would eventually stall and fade into infinity, having died. While the vehicle was moving, hidden in some cold corner of the cargo compartment of a van, Raúl Pérez felt guilty. Silently, to himself, he reproached himself for thinking about his lover, but it was inevitable. He wondered where Alicia was now, and how, starting the next day, she would be alone and helpless, just as she had always feared. He thought constantly about how she would manage, how she would survive without him. He was certain that if this was the end of his life, she would have to find someone new to live with. Even though Alicia deserved some affection for the many years she had stayed by his side, Raúl knew he had been a parasite.

He realized it had been so long since he had told anyone, "I love you." He hadn't said it to anyone, especially not Alicia. In truth, he hadn't loved her; he had needed her, used her. Eventually, a wave of pity for himself washed over him, stronger than ever before. His children came to his mind, and he felt deeply insecure about what he had meant to them. His daughter had been the closest thing to his adoration, but he had never been good at expressing it. He had spent his life moving from bed to bed, only to satisfy himself. He had assumed she knew, but now he realized he should have told her. And Fernando, he was so special to his father, but Fernando had never known it.

In silence, he asked for their forgiveness and tried to rest from the torturous agony of pointless thinking. In the end, he decided to think less; he didn't want to die regretting everything he hadn't done. But realizing he had been a terrible father, an ungrateful husband, and the most miserable human being in every sense filled him with great sorrow. Now, it hurt him because it had all ended in the most unexpected way. It was painful, and he couldn't change it. He found it absurd to think about all he had had within reach but had never bothered to take care of what was beyond his grasp.

He paid attention for a moment and realized he could hear the rain falling outside. He remembered how much he hated days like this, when the rain never stopped. He also realized he would die without anyone holding his hand to help him die peacefully, without a blessing and without anyone who knew him around. Mentally, he told himself, "Life is so damn cruel, so unfortunate and awful," thinking it with such fury that he was sure he had made some noise with his mouth. He was scared, thinking he had spoken out loud by accident, but still, he had done it. His body trembled, and his breath quickened. The afternoon was slipping away, and with it, the day was dying slowly, like someone losing their breath until finally, it stopped.

For some unknown reason, he recalled the sound of the piano in his house when his daughter used to play. That thought calmed him, and with the music came memories of when his children were young, when they played in the garden on weekends. He wondered why they had to grow up, why he had missed so much. Suddenly, images crossed his mind: his children riding horses, his wife back when she wore her hair long.

He didn't move, not even a little. He settled with these sparse images, which now felt like they belonged to someone else's life. While his mind was a whirlpool of images—perhaps without meaning—the "package" and I received a call from Yamila, instructing us to head straight to Mexico City Airport. She asked about the "package's" condition, questioning us both separately. We confirmed that he was fine, and she assured us that payment would be handled there.

The Tinaco and Chucho, who were with us in the old orange van—one of three vehicles we had to choose from—were complaining a little, but it didn't matter. Tinaco and I talked briefly about the events of the long day, mostly referencing the vehicle's condition and the weather. Chucho grumbled about the poor mechanical state of the car, and we told him to deal with it. That's how this business worked; you didn't report anything that could later be used against you.

As Tinaco drove, the young man kept an eye on the "package," making sure he didn't cause trouble. I was content to watch the city lights as night fell, while we traveled through the narrow, steep streets of the Sierra de Santa Catarina in the van. I saw people soaked in the streets, always seeming to be in a rush. I thought about each of their stories, wondering where they were headed. I imagined all this like a colony of ants defending themselves from an attack by wasps. I realized that each person carried a burden, and it seemed heavy. Some confused it with sorrow, others with pain, but then I realized that they were all grey and the same.

We continued until we reached Avenida Zaragoza. By the time we arrived, I was lost in thoughts of Yamila—thinking about her hands and her breasts, imagining her naked. I supposed if I could see her that way, I'd touch her gently. While she sighed, I'd kiss her, and she would fall into my arms. I thought about what she would do to me, her kisses, how she would trace my wounded body with her hands, with her tongue. I hoped that with that, my soul would be healed of all the pain she had caused me since that day when she had left.

Every now and then, I reminded myself that I shouldn't forget that she had abandoned me when we lived at Marbella #37. All because of a powerful man, a man who had made her his mistress. Back then, I had been consumed by jealousy, blind with rage and helplessness. But I had survived. I had kept breathing, though sometimes I doubted how much oxygen was actually reaching my lungs. Maybe I was breathing, but the vital element wasn't really there... but I overcame it.

Tinaco brought me back to reality. We both needed to watch our backs because from now on, the hardest part would come: survival and collection. By the time the sun rose the next day, we would have started a new chapter in our lives, and nothing would ever be the same again. This was something we had discussed all day, ever since we first met. He had heard of me, and I had heard of him. I looked at my partner and said:

"This, Tinaco, my friend, will be the last afternoon we see each other. It's been a pleasure to know you, and I'll never forget you." I extended my hand, and we shook it firmly.

"Mr. Pasa, it's been the greatest honor to work with you. I've learned so much." A big smile spread across his thick-lipped face. "I won't forget you either," he said sincerely.

Later, he told me that we could meet up, that wanting to do it meant being able to do it, and that it was up to us. He suggested that maybe next week, we'd have a drink together—perhaps in some cantina or one of the many dive bars around the city. Mr. Pasa. I responded by pretending we would make it happen, to make things easier...

A premonition made me instinctively reach for my belt, checking to make sure my weapon, the same Glock 17 that had been with me for so many years, was still there with me. Meanwhile, the last rays of the sun flooded the grayish sky with red and golden tinges over the city.

20. Mexico City International Airport "Benito Juárez", Mexico City. 20:05 hrs. July 30.

General Guillermo Marín knew they had to catch Yamila at the airport. The distracted Attorney General Zapata and Alejandro Harlington had deployed every possible unit to the airport, along with the airport security, which operated the security cameras and filters to prevent Yamila from escaping.

All they had on her was a brief entry record from the immigration department, showing a pale, tired, and extremely thin teenager from Argentina. Marín had a puzzle in his head, but he was missing a piece—one that, no matter how hard he tried, wouldn't come together. It wasn't available to him, nor to anyone else. Guillermo kept repeating to himself, quietly, that she was just another prostitute; how could she have gotten tangled up in this mess? He racked his brain and finally remembered that Pasa had escaped with her many years ago. Marín thought of him nostalgically, but the urgency of the situation distracted him. He couldn't figure out what to do next. He wanted to link Pasa, Yamila, and Pérez Irigoyen's father.

Indeed, it was her, the woman from that small photo in the immigration file. Marín found it hard to believe that Pasa and she were still together. He showed the photo to General Aragón, who also saw a girl, barely fourteen, with refined features. He was immediately reminded of his own daughter, the same age as the girl in the picture. How could this young girl, in just a few years, turn their world upside down? What kind of life must she have led to get to this point? Aragón asked one of the technicians at the airport's camera center if their team could recognize the woman, even if her features had changed over the years or with plastic surgery. The security staff explained that the cameras used a biometric algorithm that remained accurate, even with the passage of time or cosmetic procedures.

On the other hand, Harlington was clear about their course of action—they needed to follow her until she met with her accomplices. They couldn't arrest her before that, or they would lose the trail to the money and Pérez Irigoyen's father. The Commissioner straightened up and asked all available agents to pay attention. He told them they needed patience—if they detained the suspect in isolation, the rest of her gang would escape, and they wouldn't learn anything about the senator's father. They would continue tracking her using the airport's camera system. Ten agents would dress as civilians, blending in with the other passengers, and their mission would be to arrest the entire criminal organization. But the priority was Raúl Pérez Brito's safety.

The most advanced group of officers immediately changed into civilian clothes, put on communication devices to maintain constant surveillance and mobility, and took the precaution of arranging for an unmarked car without official insignia or sirens. They were allowed to carry their service weapons but were explicitly forbidden from firing, especially inside the airport.

Yamila's facial data was sent to the C4 center to be entered into the security system so that if she was captured by any of the cameras, an alert would trigger at the airport's C4. This would make locating and tracking her easier. Uniformed officers would wait until the undercover agents established a security perimeter before taking action.

When Harlington finished explaining this, he turned to Aragón and asked, "General, be honest with me, does any of this even make sense? I mean, you have so much experience in intelligence. From what you've seen, do you think we're on the right track?"

"It's hard to say," replied General Aragón, "but we have no choice but to continue. We have no other options and not enough time." He then looked him in the eye with great resolve. "Nothing makes sense, General. Not today, not ever."

When the generals arrived at the airport's command center, they quickly coordinated with the security team at the terminal. The guards had already uploaded Yamila's photograph and details into the suspect search programs, so it was only a matter of waiting for the technology to do its job.

It didn't take long. Suddenly, one of the computers detected the face of the Argentine woman. The alarms went off, and the system pinpointed her location within the terminal.

There she was—Yamila, coming out of an HSBC branch in the northern part of the airport. She had the same pale skin, brown hair, and blue eyes. She was heading toward Terminal 2, so they were instructed to follow her discreetly. She was constantly on the phone, as if receiving instructions through it. She was visibly nervous, and as she talked, she frequently adjusted her green skirt—her favorite color—while putting on and taking off a pair of Dolce & Gabbana sunglasses, clearly to hide her face.

How people change, thought Marín. She's no longer that fragile little girl, now she's a woman in every sense of the word. Yamila walked towards the airport lockers, where she picked up a black briefcase. She then headed back towards the parking lot, where she got into a blue BMW, and drove through the covered tunnels until reaching the lot. Six Federal Police officers, dressed in plain clothes, followed her closely, scrutinizing every step, every sway of her slender hips, every sound of her heels.

The blue vehicle she was in started, its lights flickering on, and it descended a level before driving onto the avenue beside the airport perimeter. Three patrol cars, along with a vehicle with no sirens or markings, followed her discreetly. One of the cars had an onboard camera, sending images of her actions to the C4 control center, where Marín, Aragón, and Harlington were watching everything unfold.

After traveling for over three kilometers, the blue luxury car stopped on a dark, perpendicular street. Yamila waited for a few minutes. Meanwhile, the tension at C4 increased. Harlington was unsure, insisting they should arrest Yamila and force the information out of her. However, just as the debate between the generals and him was almost settled by the Commissioner, a van arrived at the dark street.

Inside was a strong man, a young boy, and another man whom Marín instantly recognized.

Seeing him, General Guillermo Marín exclaimed, "Him! That's 'El Pasa'. Look at him, the same fool who left everything we gave him and betrayed us for that same woman."

Marín remembered how confused he had been that afternoon when "Wally" had told him that his contact had escaped with one of his girls, leaving the box empty and stealing the truck. He hadn't heard anything about the money or the man in years, but somehow, Marín knew he would see him again. He had imagined it would happen one day, but never like this, never under these conditions.

For a moment, General Guillermo Marín thought about how he owed his freedom to this man. He smiled to himself, secretly knowing that his life debt had been repaid. Harlington insisted they should arrest them right now, but both Aragón and Marín assured him they had full control over the situation. It was just a matter of waiting to find the leader or gather more information. The three men continued discussing the plan in the C4 control center.

Yamila took out her phone again and handed the briefcase she had retrieved from the airport lockers to the burly man who had gotten out of the van. He waved it away with his hands, refusing to accept it. The other man, identified by Marín as "El Pasa," shook his head as well and got back into the van. Something was going on, but from C4, they couldn't make sense of what was happening.

Journey from the Golf Club "La Hacienda" to Mexico City International Airport, 7:50 PM, July 30th.

Lucía had been instructed by her ex-sister-in-law and Fernando's mother to travel together. They were going to the house of the senator's ex-wife, just a few blocks from theirs, to pick up whatever was necessary. They even decided to escort Fernando to the airport, at least as close as possible. Lucía made a brief stop at her house, and when she left, she got back into the van with her ex-sister-in-law and ex-mother-in-law, sitting by the window on the right side. As they drove off, she could see Fernando's Mercedes Benz with him at the wheel and two patrol cars escorting him. She watched closely as the kilometers passed by, noticing that her ex-husband seemed to be talking to someone, although he was alone.

She kept watching intently, noticing that at times, Fernando would let go of the steering wheel and make hand gestures, a classic sign of when he was reprimanding someone over the phone. Who could he be talking to at that exact moment? Who was it that he couldn't have already spoken to, or couldn't talk to from the comfort of his living room?

The streets turned into rivers of red and white lights going in the opposite direction, the lamps illuminating the road as the night fell and time grew short, Lucía thought.

She glanced back at Fernando's car and thought she saw him take out his cellphone from his jacket. At that moment, Valeria's phone rang, activating the van's connection system. Now the speakers in the van broadcasted the conversation, and every gesture, every movement of his hands, aligned with every inflection of Fernando's voice.

He told his sister not to buy tickets for McAllen but for Dublin. He said the captors had contacted him and they had to take a different route, for the safety of the family. He reassured her, saying that he would return with his father no matter what.

The three women continued their journey, until, at some point, Fernando's Mercedes and its escort of federal patrols disappeared from view. They would now head to the Lufthansa counter, just as Fernando had instructed, instead of the American Airlines counter, as originally planned.

According to the plan, a delegation of officials would be waiting for them there, as Fernando's personal secretary had already purchased tickets for Texas.

Fernando Pérez Irigoyen made his way to Hangar 231, a place he had rented for years. Inside, he kept one of his most prized possessions: a Cessna 180, the plane in which he had learned to fly. He often used it to impress his conquests, sometimes flying to Acapulco for the weekend, other times for business, like the time President Trevilla invited him to join a tour in San Luis Potosí. Upon arrival, he found his father bound, his eyes covered with a black cloth. From the trunk of the Mercedes, he pulled out sacks filled with Euro bills of various denominations. Quickly, he began loading them into the plane.

Out of the shadows emerged Yamila, held at gunpoint by Tinaco. Right in front of him stood Pasa, pointing a weapon directly at him.

"Senator, it seems we aren't exactly timely," Pasa said, holding the gun against Fernando Pérez. "I must admit, it bothers me when someone refuses to pay for such a well-done job."

"Excuse me, but the payment was supposed to come from Yamila. I... I actually have other matters to attend to," Fernando said, trying to ignore the man aiming the gun at him.

"The 'payment' she's made us, this traitor, is... newspaper clippings," Pasa said, tossing a suitcase full of clipped newspaper pieces the size of bills at him. "But I won't accept this. In any case, it would be better to settle this with 'an eye for an eye, a tooth for a tooth.'"

"Please, Fernando, tell them I had no idea...," Yamila pleaded, as Tinaco yanked her by the hair, holding a revolver to her head. "Tell them I only picked up the suitcase from the lockers. I have nothing to do with its contents, please!" she cried.

Inside the plane, Pérez Irigoyen grabbed a Colt pistol. He stepped out slowly, as if searching for the right words to say to these two men. Once he had fully risen and was shielded by the aircraft, he fired at Tinaco, hitting him in the neck and knocking him to the ground. Pasa rushed to his fallen comrade, checking the wound and the blood flowing from the body of the man lying on the floor. He looked at him and said not to bother, then saw Yamila running toward the Senator. He grabbed her by the neck and aimed his gun at her, using her as a shield.

Pasa reacted in fury, rushing toward him with his gun drawn.

"So, you're... Alejandro, the Pasa?" the Senator yelled.

"I guess you know me, and I imagine you're the piece of scum that woman left me for," Pasa responded, trying to find a better angle for a shot.

"Yes, I'm the one she's always preferred, this little slut," Pérez Irigoyen said, grinning.

"No, that's not true. I've never preferred him. I prefer you... you've always been the love of my life," Yamila shouted in desperation.

"Shut up, Yamila, don't say anything. It's better if you say nothing," Alejandro Mejía snapped. "I don't want to hear you, I don't want to hear your voice, or know about you."

"But it's the truth, Alejandro! I love you, I've loved you since the day you stopped me from leaving the 'Jake Mate'... I've loved you since the first moment I knew you existed," Yamila shouted, tears streaming down her face. "Come, save me, do it for all those nights..."

"I told you to shut up! I don't want to hear your voice! I hate you, I hate you since the day you left me, since you abandoned me like a dog," Pasa said, sobbing.

"Bravo, how sweet. The criminal doesn't defend the prostitute," Fernando said, mocking Yamila as he yanked her hair. "I'm going to have to write a book about this."

He took two steps to his left, intending to circle the plane, but in the darkness, Mejía had disappeared. No matter how much the Senator searched, he couldn't find him.

"One day, many years ago, you told me, Yamila: 'What's most loved is often what's most hurt and wounded,'" Pasa said, his voice low and calm.

"Yes, love, I said that," Yamila admitted, a mix of tenderness and doubt in her voice. "But why are you saying this? Why now?"

"Because it's true," Pasa declared.

Without another word, he shot Yamila twice—once in her right thigh, and again in the liver. She screamed in pain and fell, the dead weight of her body too much for Fernando to support.

Here is the translated and improved narrative in English:

"Goodbye, love of my life, goodbye forever. Now you can leave, and as I promised you once, I have finally freed you from this damn life that you never deserved," said El Pasa, deeply affected. "Now you're free, free forever."

"I'm cold, Alejandro, I'm so scared..." came the weak, almost inaudible voice of the woman who had been left lying in a pool of blood.

"You killed her... but how? Why? She... it's impossible," Fernando said in disbelief.

Barely a moment later, a bullet pierced the skull of Senator Pérez Irigoyen. In the distance, the wail of a dozen police sirens began to sound. El Pasa removed the blindfold from Raúl Pérez Brito, who was stunned by the scene. El Pasa stepped out, ready to face the police. A shootout ensued, and he did not survive.

July 30 th, 8:12 PM - Office of the Head of Government of Mexico City, Downtown

The Head of Government gazed through the rain-soaked window at the horizon, lit up with bright lights. He looked at the Zócalo Plaza, watching the cars pass by. For a brief moment, as he observed the buildings with their lights on and the Metropolitan Cathedral in view, he thought about how the clouds consumed the sky and how the mountains in the distance seemed crowned with them. The antennas on the Chiquihuite mountain looked ridiculous, and far off in the horizon, the moon could be seen.

He picked up the red phone next to his desk, feeling an odd premonition. He asked what they knew about Senator Pérez Irigoyen's father. The voice on the other end, from one of his advisors, said they had an update. As he focused on the relentless sound of the rain, he was informed that the Senator had died. Apparently, he had been in contact with the kidnappers of his father, and when he attempted to deliver the ransom, he was shot by the captors.

A long silence stretched across the phone line. The Head of Government sat back in his chair, asked no further questions, and simply hung up the receiver.

He recalled a few days prior when he had met informally with the Senator in the private office of a mutual friend. He remembered Fernando's slow, measured walk. He had congratulated him on the progress of the reforms, especially the telecommunications reform that had been stuck in Congress for years. It had seemed impossible to get it through, but Fernando, as always, smiled and thanked him for the compliment. He looked a little tired, but that was natural; he had more work than anyone else. He had mastered politics, building a huge coalition that had accepted the risks and taken on the challenge—thanks to him.

The Head of Government recalled how Fernando had made an important remark during their conversation. He had asked if the Head of Government was preparing for a presidential run:

"Manuel, let me confess something to you: none of that. You know I'm a patriot, a servant, and nothing more. As Morelos would say, a servant, not a dictator, not someone who only seeks power. Besides, my dear friend, how many Senators have ever made it to the Presidency? Clearly, they gave me this seat so my career would end here."

The Head of Government of Mexico City remembered sighing and raising his eyebrows in agreement.

"Between us, the party wants other things. It seems they'll decide in the next few days to back one of those grandsons of the founders of Acción Católica," Fernando had said, taking a shot of tequila. "Another one of those who never connects with the electorate. You saw what happened in the State of Mexico when they sent Ruiz Echegaray's grandson to run... Well, I'm not complaining; at least I didn't get burned."

"I've thought about it," Fernando had continued. "I want to retire big, with a nice sum of money. I'm going abroad, taking Lucia, my ex-wife. I'll buy a new life, no pressure, no more of the crap here. Honestly, I'm tired and fed up with all the humiliation for not being 'one of the founders.'"

"You're leaving, Fer... where to?" the Head of Government had asked.

"I don't know, my friend, wherever. Maybe to my house in McAllen or Dublin, still no extradition," Fernando had replied sarcastically. "It's a matter of finding some good publicity..."

The Head of Government of Mexico City remembered that they had talked for a while, and their conversation had mostly revolved around the events of that horrible day in July. But they avoided talking about politics. At the end of their meeting, Fernando had said goodbye to Manuel, telling him he'd probably be the candidate for the left. He mentioned that with all his hard work, he was very close to winning. But if, for any reason, he couldn't be there to celebrate with him, he wished him the best from afar.

It was strange how clear everything had seemed at the time. That afternoon, Fernando had also said he would recover all that he had invested in politics, all the things no one had paid him back for. Those were words no one understood, especially when they saw the photograph of them taken with their arms around each other. Just minutes earlier, that photo would have been the cover of national newspapers.

For a moment, the man in the yellow-and-red tie and black suit considered telling someone that no one had been kidnapped, that it had all been orchestrated by Senator Fernando Pérez Irigoyen, right under everyone's noses. But he remembered that in politics, it's vital to hide others' problems, and besides, this took a huge burden off his shoulders for the upcoming election season. One less thing to worry about, he muttered to himself while pouring himself an old fashioned whisky.

The next morning, during his press conference, surrounded by flashes from cameras and microphones from the major TV channels, he would say, wearing a black tie:

"Last night, a patriot died. We said goodbye too soon to someone who was like a brother to me, a model brother, a brave son, a dear friend. The death of Fernando Pérez Irigoyen has shaken us, destroyed us, and deeply moved us. He died at the hands of cruel, cowardly, and vile criminals—enemies of the State—with whom he fought face to face every day, relentlessly, his entire life. He did it with bravery, with gallantry, just as he was.

In our memories, we will remember a just man who fought for the ideals of the Mexican nation. A man who chose his own death rather than corrupting himself. May his sacrifice remind us all, without distinction, of the legitimate interests of our people. May his death not be in vain and may it open a new chapter in the fight against the insecurity and violence that have taken over our beloved country.

Rest in peace, my friend, Senator Fernando Pérez Irigoyen, an exceptional patriot."

www.ingramcontent.com/pod-product-compliance
Ingram Content Group UK Ltd.
Pitfield, Milton Keynes, MK11 3LW, UK
UKHW042153171224
452513UK00001B/75